the BAGMAN vs.
THE WORLD'S FAIR

B.C. Bell

AIRSHIIP 27 PRODUCTIONS

Editor: Ron Fortier
Associate Editor: Gordon Dymowski
Marketing and Promotions: Micael Vance

Cover © 2013 Laura Givens
Interior illustrations © 2013 Andy Fish
Prouction and design by Rob Davis

An Airship 27 Production
www.airship27.com
www.airship27hangar.com

ISBN-13: 978-0615875620
ISBN-10: 0615875629

Printed in the United States of America

10 9 8 7 6 5 4 3 2 1

the BAGMAN vs. THE WORLD'S FAIR

Prologue

From the Files of Detective Jake Costanovitch,
Chicago Police Department

Name: McCullough, Francis "Mac" *--No known middle name*
Born: Cook County, Illinois, September 3, 1908
Parents: James McCullough--construction contractor
(deceased), Margaret McCullough--housewife, (Allen, Texas).

Height: 6 feet.
Weight: 190 lbs.
Hair color: Brown/Copper
Eyes: Blue
Known aliases: About a hundred different pro ballplayers.
Suspected Aliases: Melvin Stratford (New York), David Polidori
(Kansas City), Artaugh Singh (Philadelphia), Lefty Grove (Salem,
Pennsylvania)

Note: characteristics and operating methods of suspect
unconfirmed. McCullough also fits profile of masked criminal/
vigilante THE BAGMAN.
*-BUT McCullough's a CAREER criminal!?? His whole
history involves professional profit!*

1921: Thirteen-year-old Frank "Mac" McCullough's father found
dead in Lake Michigan. Assumed drowned.

1922: Age 14, McCullough escapes from several foster parents and
an orphanage. Is arrested for vagrancy in Detroit. Becomes a hobo.
Last seen hopping a train in Michigan.

1921—1931: There are no records of McCullough's whereabouts for
ten years. See: Possible Aliases.

April 1931: Age 24, McCullough returns to Chicago. Is questioned
concerning rash of burglaries, confidence games, and his
involvement with the "Slots" Lurie Gang.

May '33: Drops out of sight. First sighting of THE BAGMAN—takes gang hostage with hand grenade at corner grocery 3600 Southport. One week later "Slots" Lurie found dead inside the wreckage of his own speakeasy headquarters. Evidence left by THE BAGMAN reveals Mac's Father to have been poisoned, twelve years ago, most likely by "Slots" Lurie.

June '33: Suspect opens "Mac's Tobacco" shop on Lincoln Ave. No visible crime links. THE BAGMAN involved in arrest of alleged Chicago Police torture ring.

June '33: McCullough still rents apartment on north side, missing for three weeks.

--Half the lowlifes in town know this bastard. Who the hell is he?

Chapter One
1933: THE FORTUNE OF JULY

The city of Chicago was bankrupt. Everybody else was just broke.

The Great Depression held America in a death grip, while Prohibition still wobbled on its last legs refusing to die. Mae West had just beaten Cagney at the box-office—but King Kong was about to get taken out by a five-year-old named Shirley Temple. Fascism reared its head in Europe, and America was in the middle of a crime wave. The world was upside down, changing too fast, and—as always—on the verge of extinction.

Despite all that, American industry had entered a new age of invention. Lighting, film, automobile, telephone, telegraph, radio and aviation industries were changing the world.

It was an age of science, an age of wonder.

Yet, without the darkness, there would be no light.

The pitch black was ignited by the scrape and flash of a wooden match. The flame in the darkness displayed the hand holding it. The hand holding it lit a fuse. The gunpowder in the fuse popped and crackled as the flame crossed the gravel floor of the room.

"Three…Two…One…Go!"

Tommy "The Machine" Ahearn hit the button on top of his stopwatch and ducked. The concrete wall on the other side of the bunker in front of him exploded.

Tommy's head popped around the barricade, and a tough guy carrying a sledgehammer burst through the darkness in the tunnel behind him. Tommy smiled, still staring at the stopwatch's face like the ticking hand was about to reveal his fate.

Only Tommy The Machine didn't believe in fate. He believed in precision. Fine tuned, well-oiled, inhuman, clinical precision.

For the last three years Ahearn had been traveling the country, robbing seemingly random banks from coast to coast and he'd been working on

The First State Bank of Illinois for over three months. He'd memorized the floor plan, hours, and employees. Every aspect of security. He knew what time the big deposits went in, when the courier came, the cop on the beat's schedule and, most importantly, he knew they didn't have a night watchman on duty tonight.

Had Tommy been less of a serious-minded individual, he might have laughed at the fact that the bank trusted their new alarm system so much. But Tommy The Machine's sense of humor had died about the same time his ability to play had, leaving him like a musician who can only perform what's written on the sheet music. Which is part of what made him so dangerous.

Not that Tommy didn't have a back up plan for every possible occurrence—he did, but there remained that one big threat: If the rest of the band didn't play along, he'd smash all the instruments.

And kill the entire audience.

If things didn't work out, people would die.

For the past two weeks, Tommy and his gang had been digging a tunnel that led from the basement of a three-flat, under a back alley, to a mere thirteen inches away from the inside of the First State Bank's vault. Each and every man in Ahearn's crew of five had been instructed, drilled, tested and could repeat their part of the plan by rote. Then, a week ago everything had almost fallen apart. One of the crew, Tops Carter, disappeared.

Tommy had called everyone in the gang to a meeting in their basement headquarters and threatened them at gunpoint. When the threats didn't work, he made an announcement.

"'If the plan isn't working, it won't.' That's my motto. I'm calling the job off."

Unfortunately for the bank, the underworld deals in shadow, rumor, and a never-ending line of desperate men. And one of the desperate men in Ahearn's gang just happened to know about another shadowy man in that never-ending line.

"Boilermaker" Bill McCoy had just barely fit the bill. Standing six-feet tall and broad shouldered, Bill could just fit in the tunnel. A couple of old timers from the O'Banyon mob had vouched for him and while his background seemed more in the armed robbery department, the fact that he'd evidently been working a few long con games revealed him as a man who could keep a secret. Bill had answered all of Ahearn's questions correctly, and immediately done whatever he was told. He didn't talk much and despite a barb-wire, handlebar mustache, and a taste for loud sport coats, he seemed like a smart guy.

Smart. But not too smart.

Then again, McCoy had mentioned that it wasn't really all that hard to buy a house under an assumed name, and then proceeded to explain how to do it. It took awhile, but that's probably what motivated Ahearn to announce the bank job was back on. After all, if he didn't finish it, this "Boilermaker" Bill McCoy just might.

After the explosion, a dustbowl filled the small room at the end of the tunnel, but the shadowy figures in the murk moved with a purpose. An industrial fan switched on and began sucking the dirty air down the tunnel behind them.

Boilermaker Bill picked up a sledgehammer in one hand and a crowbar in the other. He stepped up the line, around Tommy The Machine and approached the steel wall.

"I think we already got it," Boilermaker Bill said, dropping the crowbar in the dirt. The big man slid his hands along the sledgehammer's handle, and started striking down the sharp metal edges sticking out of the hole in the safe wall.

Once the edges were blunt enough to crawl inside the safe, Tommy The Machine waved an arm. Two smaller men with flashlights advanced from the rear. Ahearn went in first; he had a list of safety deposit box numbers that was likely to pay more than the rest of the haul. The two smaller men climbed in behind him. Boilermaker Bill and a Frenchman named Pinter remained outside in the tunnel.

Once the loot was handed off from the safe, Bill and Frenchy would shuttle it underground and back to the basement across the alley. Tommy's list of safety deposit boxes and the fortunes therein were to be handed out last. That and the fact that the rest of Tommy's gang would hunt them down and kill them, guaranteed that Bill and the Frenchman wouldn't try to grab part of the take and run.

Tommy's miniature penlight pierced the darkness inside the vault, a circle of light scanning the money lined walls. As the two lightweight men climbed in behind him, The Machine did something human.

He whistled like he'd seem a pretty girl, only more. Like he'd seen the goddess Venus, and he was trying to hail her a cab. Loud and shrill, it echoed down the tunnel.

Bill and Frenchy, waiting for somebody to hand them a bag of bills, anxiously shifted their feet outside and looked at each other with lowered eyebrows. It was the first time anybody in the gang had ever heard The Machine laugh.

And it wasn't pretty.

It was creepy, Doctor Frankenstein creepy, like any minute he was going to start yelling "It's aliiiiiive!" and lightening would erupt from every savings account in the city.

It didn't, but Bill stepped a little farther back anyway. It seemed natural because even if they hadn't been underground, the noise would have been deafening, especially once they started wrenching the safety deposit boxes from the wall.

Inside the vault, metal hit metal. Metal bent and split. Every hammer banged short and steady. A shearing sound ended with a clip, and the safety deposit box drawers would clatter as they were torn off their rails. Only to be followed by a moment of dry paper shuffling and the occasional rattle of family treasures, stocks, bonds, and deeds.

All of it falling like autumn leaves into two-foot tall moneybags, just waiting to be hoisted away.

Three minutes later, a black sleeve popped from the inside of the safe wall. The fist at the end of the sleeve opened, and a bagful of money dropped on the floor. Then another.

Boilermaker Bill didn't move. The moneybags weren't the large size, and the two "mules" were supposed to carry three at a time. Tomorrow being Sunday, they still had twenty-four hours to empty the safe but the plan was to do it in two, and put plenty of space between them and Chicago before Monday. The Frenchman carried the first load of money out. Bill didn't move. He was supposed to wait for the next load. The route back to the three-flat wasn't torturous, but they hadn't had time to level the floors so they were given eight minutes for each run.

Three more money bags dropped out to of the iron hole in the wall. Boilermaker didn't even shift his feet.

The Frenchman came out of the darkness behind him, crouching in the dim light. When he saw the moneybags on the floor he almost screamed.

"Sacre Bleu! Why are you not moving, Bill? The Machine will have our heads!"

"Whoa, whoa there, Frenchy," Bill said. "It's all part of the plan."

"I know the plan..." The Frenchman began fidgeting with his fingers and going down his memorized list. "One, we dull the edges of the hole with the sledgehammer. Two, we carry the loot by threes back to the basement..."

"Change of plans, Pinter."

"Oh, my God!" Frenchy bit his lip. "Why are we not running?"

"Don't panic. The Machine's got a back up. He wants to talk to you."

The Frenchman's knees wiggled and the back of his hand swept across his forehead in a martyr's salute.

Bill smiled. "Don't worry. Everything's aces. I think he came across a French document, wants to know what it is."

"He knows this is not the time! The..." Frenchy stopped himself before insulting the boss. "We'll sort through the papers later!" Pinter flexed his shoulders as he approached the wall and stuck his head in the vault.

Up until he stuck his head in the wall, no one in the vault had been able to hear what was going on outside. Tommy The Machine looked up from a safety deposit box and spotted Frenchy blocking the light. Tommy's entire face widened in surprise and then narrowed in adulterated hate.

That's when Boilermaker Bill moved.

Frenchy Pinter felt something grab him by the back of the collar and under his belt. He flew into the vault like a tossed banana peel, his head colliding with one of the other gangsters before he rolled onto the floor.

From outside, a Colt snubnose revolver fired three, deafening shots inside the vault. Everybody froze.

"Anybody comes out of the hatch gets it," a voice that wasn't Boilermaker Bill's said. He was already stacking the five moneybags behind the barricade in front of the tunnel.

Tommy The Machine's eyes went wide and darted from one man to the other entombed with him in the safe. This wasn't part of the plan.

"You're dead, Bill! Dead!" he screamed and jerked a .38 automatic out of his shoulder holster.

The revolver outside the hole cracked again. Tommy grabbed his shoulder, pirouetted in a nasty circle and fell over the Frenchman. The rest of the gangsters' eyes darted around the vault like they were looking for another exit.

"He still alive?" the voice outside said.

"I think," one of the crew said.

"I hadn't planned on that," said the voice. "Anything else comes out of that vault, there's gonna be some lead flying in."

"But, Bill," Frenchy said from the floor. "There's ten times that money in here. Why...?"

"Tell Tommy the second rule of burglary is improvisation."

Even the fallen men exchanged glances with each others. Outside, Bill was dragging the moneybags toward the tunnel entrance. Frenchy regained his feet and stuck his face back into the room at the tunnel's end. A dirt clod smacked him in the face and the voice outside continued:

"Tell Tommy a heist is like a wedding; no matter how hard you plan, it ain't gonna be like that."

Frenchy wiped the dirt from his face and chanced another glance out of the hole from behind the wall. Boilermaker Bill's broad shoulders stood out in silhouette as he shuffled across the small room to stand in the middle of it. Bill pulled something out of his jacket and stuck it in a hole in the ceiling.

Then lit the fuse.

Frenchy ducked and sidestepped the hole as the tunnel outside collapsed around them.

Frank "Mac" McCullough, who'd been a bagman for the local Chicago Outfit only a month ago, threw the moneybags on a blanket and dragged them behind him down the tunnel. Only a month ago one of Mac's business associates, a man he barely knew, had ordered him to break his uncle's legs. Mac broke his associate's nose instead. Since then he'd taken out a local mob boss, a hitman, and ring of torturers pretending to be policemen. All the wrong people on both sides of the law had papers out on Mac's alias. The mob had contracts, the cops had warrants. But something kept compelling Mac to put the mask back on.

He made it to the basement four minutes flat.

Chapter Two
THE HELLFIGHTER

By the time he had loaded the loot into Tommy's car, it was four in the morning. Mac drove to a soup kitchen, snuck in the back door and left a bag of cash in the sink. Parking the car in a back alley, he carried part of the swag upstairs to his apartment and then went back outside and parked the stolen sedan in front of a Woolworth's two blocks away.

After bacon and eggs at the five-and-dime, he left the breakfast counter and made his way to the phone booth. The temperature was beginning to climb already, and he was glad the fan in the ceiling worked when he closed the door in the booth. He shoved a nickel in the slot and picked up the earpiece.

"Operator, I need a Jacob Costanovitch on Surf Street. Yes, that's right, Detective…" There was a long pause. "Costanovitch? *Detective* Costanovitch? Yeah, I got a case for you. One maybe even you coppers can solve… Mmmmmm, could be." He sounded like a cartoon character. "Now, now, Detective, vigilante this, vigilante that. You want to solve a crime? There're four yeggs robbing the Illinois State Bank as we speak. You might want to put a couple of patrol cars on it."

The beehive sounds in the earpiece erupted into non-stop cursing.

"Get to work." Mac slammed the earpiece back on the prongs and smiled. Costanovitch would explode when he found out the bank robbers were already trapped in the safe and not in the act.

After a shower, Mac took his time shaving off the mustache, enjoying it. He'd been Boilermaker Bill for the better part of three weeks and was glad to see him go. He hadn't minded growing the hair over his lip, but he'd had to wear fake front teeth and felt like he'd been talking through a grill all month. Later that day, he would remember shaving, but not falling asleep.

Sleep was just part of the problem. He hadn't been sleeping at all, but now he'd discovered that when he did, he'd started sleepwalking again.

To sleep, perchance to dream.

But all he remembered were the nightmares. The policeman showing him the bloated dead body of his father. Running away from foster care.

Running away from the orphanage. Stealing food to eat. Learning to steal other things so he wouldn't have to steal food. His first burglary and his first long con where the victims served themselves up like moths to a flame back when life seemed to make sense.

Even if he knew it was a dream, he couldn't wake himself up. Until every crime he'd ever committed led right back to the death of his father, the same way it had in real life. When Mac had returned to the city, he'd ended up working for the same men who'd killed his dad, not that he had known it, and he'd been forced to don a mask.

There was never a mask in the nightmare.

When he woke up it was afternoon. He dampened a cloth, and wiped the cold sweat off his body. Then Mac put on his best, blue, summer suit, grabbed his hat and made for the door.

Ten minutes later, he was sauntering up Lincoln Avenue and stopping in front of Saint Alphonsus Church. He glanced around to make sure nobody was looking, and forced as big a wad of hundred dollar bills as he could into the poor box, hammering it into the slot with the back of his fist. He stuck his hands in his pockets and started sauntering again, till he'd been around the block and come up behind the car he'd just stolen from Tommy The Machine. Looked like he had some business with Crankshaft.

❈ ❈ ❈

Beneath the shadows of the elevated train on the corner of Addison and Lincoln, behind a faded yellow hot dog stand at the end of an alley that goes nowhere, sat an easily overlooked, almost vacant lot. Behind the slatted wooden fence, used automobiles sat in a row blocking the front of the lot. The back was littered with parts and frames from the corpses of a thousand cars. And sitting in the middle was an old tin shack. The sort of property a hundred people passed every day and didn't notice, except for one thing.

In the middle of the alley over the door of the gate hung a sign that read, *Crankshaft's Car Repair and Sales*. It was a nice sign, but there were a thousand others just like it in the city. No, what stood out was the sign above it. A graphic depicting an American doughboy from the Great War charging over a ribbon that read: *369th Infantry Division*.

The 369th, better known as The Harlem Hellfighters; the hardest fighting division on the Western Front. Antoine "Crankshaft" Jones had been a hero overseas; the French had even seen fit to award him their Medal of Honor, the *Croix De Guerre*. But when he got back home he was just another black man. He'd had some trouble readjusting to Harlem, and somehow wound up in Chicago. Business was all word of mouth, and business was good because anyone that knew anything about engines knew Crankshaft Jones.

Mac pulled up in Tommy's crème colored sedan and left it idling in the alley. Elated, but still tired, he was glad he didn't have to pick the padlock on Crankshaft's gate this time. It had become a game they played. Crankshaft kept changing the padlocks, and Mac kept opening them.

Mac pulled the car past the tin-scrap shack, around some piles of junk as tall he was, and into an underground garage hidden behind the detritus. Mac had started out calling the garage "the Secret Subway" because he thought Chicago needed one but now they just called it "the garage." The garage had been built without permits and was evolving into a small laboratory and warehouse. Crankshaft's side stood obsessively neat with tools hung laterally in rows and cars parked all at the same angle. Mac's side was a mish mash of books, magazines, some chemistry supplies he didn't quite know how to use yet, a folding cot and, of course, guns and ammo.

The lean and wiry Crankshaft strode like the soldier he was down the ramp into the garage, crescent wrench in one hand, handkerchief in the other. Normally, Crankshaft would have snuck up on Mac, since he was one of the few people who could do it. Instead, he smiled at the car and caught himself, then lowered his eyes and glowered critically.

"Look, Crank!" Mac waved his hand over the sedan like he'd seen a girl do in a car show one time. "A brand new car!"

"Where the hell have you been?" Crankshaft wiped the sweat from his graying temple and put the handkerchief in the pocket of his coveralls. "Been trying to get in touch with you for a month now. Even went down to that wharf-rat bar on the piers looking for you."

"The Straying Anchor? Crank, nobody, especially you, should ever go into that place. Not only will the clientele kill you, but Mickey the owner is a worse bigot than his customers. Talks about lynching like he likes it."

"Yeah, it was interesting. Place got kind of quiet when I walked in but we came to agreement."

"You what?"

"Yeah, when Mickey gets out of the hospital, we agreed I wouldn't sleep with his daughter, and he wouldn't burn a cross on my lawn. So where have you been?"

"After we took out that gang of crooked cops last month, it suddenly occurred to me they have the biggest gang in town. Thought I ought to lay low for awhile. Remember that mustache I was growing?"

"The one a quart of Brylcreem couldn't hold down?"

"Well, I was growing it for a reason." Mac walked over to Tommy's car, opened the trunk, and with the flourish of a stage magician jerked the blanket away to reveal several moneybags. "Part-time work. It pays, and nobody sees either of me."

They unloaded the swag, and hid it one of the compartments in the concrete walls, while Mac told Crankshaft about his two weeks as Boilermaker Bill, and the fifteen-to-twenty years Tommy's gang would be serving.

"They're lucky," Mac said, "I got a feeling bank-robbing is gonna be a federal offense pretty soon."

"Look, I know you think you're some kind of Lon Chaney with the disguises and stuff," Crankshaft said. "But a mustache does not a disguise make. What are you going to do when they start asking questions about where Mac McCullough was?"

"Oh, Crank, old man, what am I going to do with you?" Mac's voice dripped mock concern. "I'm sure if you check the official records, you'll find that Frank 'Mac' McCullough has been hospitalized at Cook County for the past two days and, that Hunts Helms, city reporter, turned in a story about him being hit by a car last week. Now the newspapers didn't think it was important then…"

"But you're alibied out the wazoo."

"Even that has an alibi."

"Well, nice as that may be, I don't," Crankshaft said. "I've got to get back upstairs before somebody starts wondering where I went."

They headed up top.

✳ ✳ ✳

Crankshaft's office and upstairs garage were a miracle of makeshift engineering. A stack of sheath-tin metal signs and two-by-fours that leaned when the wind blew, but never fell over. The ace mechanic pulled open the screen door, and it squeaked with a volume that the soundman on a horror radio show would have envied. He beat Mac to the desk chair and looked out the west window, then tore a page out of a newspaper and impaled it on a nail above the sash, to act as a curtain.

"Well, I'm glad you finally got my message, it's going to be a big night." Crankshaft said.

"Yeah…uh, big."

"You have no idea what I'm talking about do you?"

"Not a clue."

"The World's Fair and Exposition, my friend!"

"Aw, Crank, I don't think…" Mac wagged his head, looking at the floor.

"You haven't even been there yet."

"I went there opening day," Mac said.

"Didn't make it past the beer gardens, did you?"

"No."

One of the biggest things the World's Fair had going for it was that, thanks to a loophole in Prohibition laws, it was legal to drink there. Federal Law had declared the beer gardens on all four corners of the Fair as international zones of ambassadorship. It was the only place in the United States a person could legally buy an alcoholic beverage. People planned entire vacations around it.

"And, if I were to go again," Mac said. "Who's to say I won't just sit down and start enjoying all that diplomatic immunity all over again?"

"I will." Crankshaft unzipped his coveralls, grabbed a suit hanging on a nail by the door, and headed back toward the slop sink to wash up.

"Nah, I'm too tired," Mac said, not bothering to get up.

"Look, all you have to do is go into the actual fairgrounds with me. Once you get inside you can go home if you want to but I know you're going to flip for all that weird science and culture stuff. Besides, the only reason we're going is because Coco's going to be singing."

Coco Blue was a New York torch singer with a voice so sultry it melted glass instead of shattering it. Her looks made it glow. When Mac had first put on the mask, he and Crankshaft had saved Coco's life. Since then, Coco had stayed in Chicago and was quickly becoming Crankshaft's number one girl. One of the few things the two men could agree on was their affection for her.

Mac didn't really want to go, but something told him he should be there for Coco. That, and the tiniest tug of his subconscious.

"What time's she go on?"

"Five or six o'clock. It's a shindig for the champagne crowd."

"Well, let's go then," Mac said, kicking the door open. It swung back and forth, fighting its own springs as the invading light of the outside world swelled within the room, collapsed, and then swallowed the two figures.

Chapter Three
AMERICA'S MOST WANTED

In times of no hope people look to the future. So when Wall Street crashed in '29, the city fathers of Chicago, along with the world's greatest inventors and industrialists, came up with an idea. Not just another World's Fair, but the largest exposition of science and industry ever gathered in the history of the world.

It worked. The World's Fair rolled in the dough. People knew a good thing when they saw it and what they saw was stunning.

A quarter mile of Lake Michigan, from 12th to 39th street, 427 acres of lakeshore property had been transmogrified into a celebration of the city's centennial and the world. On opening night, light from the star Arcturus, collected from photocells in astronomical observatories all over the globe, was suddenly transformed into electrical energy. When the power hit the lights, fifteen-thousand more tiny stars shined their light on the designs of a brand new future. An "Emerald City" by the lake.

Beneath those lights, even more lights. Eight miles of neon tubing completed the effect, outlining eighty-two miles of exhibits, and more than fifty buildings with more than five-hundred displays.

And while The Sky Ride stretched across all that acreage dwarfing a Ferris Wheel whose designs had amazed the world some forty years before, the other attractions on the Midway were as down and dirty as any back alley carnival. Only, just like everything else at the fair, more so.

At an opening-event gala, an out of work burlesque dancer had managed to sneak into the club, on a horse, naked and posing as Lady Godiva. While some of the partygoers were appalled, most were delighted, and soon Sally Rand had become an international sensation. Men came from all over the world to watch Sally do her "bubble dance," a striptease performed with large clear balloons. Moralists squawked, but there was nothing they could do. Sally was world popular.

And compared to some of the peep shows on the Midway, Sally's act was tame. So much so, that at one point the French Ambassador asked to have their flag removed from the Streets of Paris exhibit.

Hall of Science be damned, thought Mac. *I'm running to see the bubble dance the second Coco finishes singing.*

Crankshaft hummed Duke Ellington's "Take the A-Train" as they paid a dime each to do just that. They hopped a streetcar for a nickel, lined up at the window and then laid down fifty cents for a ticket to see the world.

Inside the fair gate, Mac, the broad-shouldered, level headed veteran of a thousand crimes and punishments, lost all pretense of cool, calm and collectedness. Yes, this straight faced demon of law and lawlessness, this grim witness to the million tragedies of man, did something no mob boss or chief of detectives would ever be strong enough to do.

He broke out in a kid's smile. He spun, dancing an Irish jig turned soft-shoe, and finished the step with his hands spread like a vaudevillian. Turning to face Crankshaft as the mechanic came up behind him, Mac let go with a whoop loud enough to scare the children at Fort Dearborn into thinking there might be a cavalry raid.

Crankshaft grabbed him by the arm and pulled him to the side. "An hour ago you didn't even want to come here, and now you're dancing in the streets?"

"Lookatthisplace."

"They've been building it here for a year now. You pass by it almost every day."

"That's just it, Crank. I pass it by." Mac eyed the art deco horizon surrounding him, his chiseled profile turning slowly, cutting the rays of the setting sun as he saw the fair for the first time from the inside. Sure, he'd seen the newsreels, the postcards, and magazine articles but talk was cheap.

And it looked like more than what they'd said. Like some futuristic version of Alice in Wonderland.

Beneath the spectacle of the Midway's rides, the smell of popcorn, cotton candy, and sawdust were in the air. Within Mac's direct view were China, the Crown Food Company, India, the Doughnut Machine Corporation, and the Old Heidelberg Inn. Making it all the more surreal was the fact that Crankshaft, the ace mechanic, stood framed by the Firestone Tire Building behind him. Mac almost shook his head.

Crankshaft slapped him on the shoulder before he had a chance. "C'mon, we're running late. Show starts at five." He pointed at a fairgrounds bus coming to a stop down the path.

"Don't you want to walk down the Avenue of Flags?" Mac said.

"And walk a half mile out of my way? I've seen flags before; besides, they're all red. And we don't have time to be late for the gala presentation."

Mac glanced at some of the rickshaw drivers.

Crankshaft ignored him and sat down in back of the open air bus. Mac hopped on next to him, but remained standing so he could look around as they traveled. A confused look formed on his face as the bus passed the Old Morocco club, where unknowns like Judy Garland and The Andrews

Sisters were being discovered every night. He'd thought Coco would be playing there, but Crankshaft didn't bother to get off for two more stops. And even then he just kept walking south.

Mac managed not to say anything until they were standing in front of Frank Buck's Jungle Camp. A troop of monkeys loitered on a series of landings behind a wire fence across from them. Mac could think of street corners in town where the little primates wouldn't have looked out of place.

"Uh, Crank, Coco didn't get the short end of the stick did she?"

"What do you mean?"

"I thought we were going to the Old Morocco. I was kind of hoping this might be her big shot."

"Oh, she's shooting for the moon tonight, Mac. Not some dingy night club." Crankshaft stopped in the middle of the path and pointed to a gigantic band shell aimed toward the lake.

"Whoa, she's playing for the Mayor's Medal Presentation?" Mac didn't know what the Mayor's Medal Presentation was, but he knew it was a big deal. They'd been promoting it in the papers for months, and there were signs all over the place. Apparently seating required an extra ticket purchase.

"Here's your ticket." Crankshaft slapped a chit into Mac's palm.

"Aw, Crank, you know I don't need that." Mac stopped, frozen in the middle of the path, staring at a policeman having his picture taken with a tourist.

"Yes, you will, unless you're some kind of ambassador or something. They got this place sealed tight. It's going to be wall to wall celebrities, heroes, inventors, royalty…"

"Yeah, royalty…" Mac kept staring at the tourist and the cop; paying no attention to Crankshaft at all. He was shuffling away backwards before he said, "I'll be right back, Crank. I got to talk to this guy."

Crankshaft shrugged and headed over to a soda stand for a bottle of Coke. He'd seen Mac get that look before. He decided to wait and leaned against the side of the wooden booth, sipping his soda, watching.

Mac shuffled forward now, hands in pockets, hat tilted back. The tourists consisted of two young women, and a well groomed man wearing a straw boater and a two-hundred dollar suit. It had been tailored so the gun in his shoulder holster wouldn't show.

The women, one in a brown dress, one in red, wore real pearls and were taking pictures of their friend and a patrolman with a brand new Kodak Brownie, tossing the little brown box back and forth like it was a toy. The man in the expensive suit held his jacket draped over one shoulder, his other arm patting the cop on the back as they posed. The two men finished and shook hands. Then, smiling and chuckling to himself, the man in the straw hat headed back toward the two attractive photographers. He was about to wrap an arm around each of them, when something grabbed him by the wrist.

"John, we got to talk," Mac said.

"Name's not John, kid. It's Jake." The man shot him a neighborly smile.

The blonde woman in red tried to sound angry. "Yeah, he ain't who you're looking for, bub!"

"It's not Jake, it's John." Mac's eyes narrowed, but his expression was unreadable. "I know it. You know it."

"Get outta here, mister!" The squeaky-voiced blonde grated, "Or I'll call that cop back here! He'll let you have what for!"

"No, I don't think so." Mac hadn't broken eye contact with "Jake."

"You don't think I'll do it! Why you four-flushing..." She raised two fingers to her mouth and whistled.

Mac felt the man tense in his grip.

"I didn't mean you wouldn't call a cop." Mac acknowledged the blonde for the first time. "I meant the cop's not going to let me have 'what for.' Especially, when he finds out 'Jake' here, isn't Jake."

Sweat dripped in the man's mustache, but he kept smiling as his head veered between Mac and the woman in red. The policeman turned around and started walking back.

Mac released his grip. The man stood frozen.

"It's alright, officer," the man in the boater said. "Just ran into an old friend, trying to get his attention."

The cop smiled and headed in the other direction, stopping in the center of a crosswalk a hundred yards away.

"'Scuse me, ladies," Mac said. "'Jake' and I need to talk a little business."

The blonde's lip twitched in anger. Mac gave her a wink, grabbed the man by the crook of his arm and pulled him off the pathway next to the jungle exhibit. The man in the boater glanced over each shoulder, making sure nobody was behind him. Then, they faced each other eye to eye. Two predators, one sizing up the other.

The man's hand hovered in front of the lapel by his shoulder holster.

"Don't be stupid, John. You shoot here, there are witnesses and even more cops. Neither of us wants that."

"I told you once already, mister. My name's not John. It's Jake; Jake Dillon."

"Wow! Even your alias stinks, John."

The man's teeth bared in a manner that would have made Frank Buck's jungle animals proud. "You calling me a liar?"

"I'm calling you John."

There was a long silence. "Look, mister. I got five hundred dollars on me.

"Don't be Stupid, John."

It's yours if you'll just keep quiet."

"I don't want your money, just a word."

The man looked down at his shoes, then back up at Mac.

"John." Mac paused, this time without protest. "You may think it's cute taking pictures with the cops, making fun of the chumps, but you're forgetting something. You can laugh all you want at the corn-fed rubes back home but this ain't Indiana. It's Chicago."

The man glared silently, knives shooting from his eyes underneath the straight brim of his straw hat.

"Chicago will kill you, John. If the cops don't get you, the mobsters will just for bringing in more heat. I hear they got a nice deal going on with the mayor in St. Paul right now; hideouts and the cops are paid for. You should check Minnesota out."

"Jake's" mouth cracked like he had to work to keep his jaw from falling open. Another moment of silence.

"That all you want?" the man said.

"It's not me, John, Jake, whatever your name is, it's you. This city'll kill ya."

"OK..." The man broke eye contact, shrugged his shoulders. "Well, thanks. I guess..." He actually held out his hand. Mac took it.

"And get another alias. Really, I can understand wanting to keep your initials and all, but Dillon? It's just too close."

The man's fists clamped even tighter at his sides. "Are we done?"

"Get out of town." Mac gave "Jake" a friendly punch on the shoulder and smiled for the policeman in the distance's benefit. "And watch out for that broad in red. She's trouble."

The cop still watched from down the path, twirling his nightstick by the leather cord around his wrist.

"You should use some of that money for a trip on the Sky-Ride before you go!" Mac hollered, waving. "This could be your last chance."

He strolled over to the refreshment stand where Crankshaft was finishing his soda pop. "Jake" stood where he'd been, staring blankly into space. The girl in brown put a hand on "Jake's" arm, and he forced a smile onto his face that didn't look quite right.

"Old friend?" Crankshaft asked, mulling over his empty, green bottle.

"More of a business acquaintance."

"Looks kind of familiar."

"You might have seen him in the papers; name's Dillinger."

They watched as the man walked off with a girl under each arm, headed for the auditorium band shell and the Mayor's Medal Ceremony.

"So, Crank, you were saying...? About all that royalty that's supposed to be showing up..."

Crankshaft sighed and started walking toward the band shell. "Leave it to you to spot the gangster in the crowd."

"Hey, over there by the balloon rides…" Mac pointed. "…isn't that Pretty Boy Floyd?"

Chapter Four
THE EXPLODING AMBASSADOR

Mac was glad they had tickets when he saw the set up. The band shell sat next to the Hollywood Exhibit facing the lake, where the ceremony could be recorded on film. And while the only things keeping the riff raff out were ushers and a four-foot tall fence, the open air meant everybody was a witness. Sitting in the third row next to Crankshaft, Mac decided the best way to crash the gate would be to wait until after the show started.

Even as a guest he was still figuring out how to break in.

The place was packed, and it was a ritzy crowd; half of them already in evening wear, and the rest in their Sunday best. The evening award ceremony was to be followed by the ritual lighting of The Century of Progress, when it truly would become a city of electric light, to be followed by a night of music, celebration and dance. Night going into morning.

The highly regarded and upright crowd almost made Mac a bit uncomfortable. Not that he had anything against respectability; it was just too easy to fake. Crankshaft's eyes were glued to the curtains like he knew exactly where Coco Blue would appear.

The rattles and waves of scattered noise from the musician's tuning broke into the familiar hum of one note, then into a silence that caused the crowd to hush. The curtain raised and a man behind a podium asked if the crowd would please rise for the national anthem.

But the band had an opening. Even as the announcer spoke they'd been playing three ascending chords, repeating them. The moment his voice stopped, the three notes repeated, and a vocal blended with them to sing, "O-oh, sa-ay can you seeee." Something in the percussion section kick-started the backbeat. The rhythm shifted into fourth gear, and a pair of brushes massaged the melody down till every sound had become one.

Coco appeared where Crankshaft had been staring all along.

She came up out of the stage like Venus on the half-shell. Near-invisible stage lights highlighted the sheen of her coffee colored skin, and contrasted with the white evening gown and burlesque skullcap on her head. The outfit shined, resplendent with a thousand tiny rhinestones reflecting the still invisible lights. Her voice seemed to pull the band along with it, supporting everything until a phrase, or note delayed, stretched on its musical frame like tapestry on a loom.

Crankshaft's eyes hadn't moved.

By the "dawn's early light," even the folks in line at the concession stands had turned around to pay attention. By "the twilight's last gleaming," the city fathers and representatives had stopped looking confused by the musical arrangement and started to share smiles with the rest of the world. Some Chicago aldermen may not have thought Jazz was an American treasure, but the foreign diplomats understood it for what it was, a distinctly original American sound. By "the home of the brave," Coco had not only won a standing ovation, but a rave review from Chicago, and the world.

Mac stood up on his chair to applaud. The normally stoic Crankshaft stood with the rest of the crowd, clapping, and whistling loud enough to signal boats on the Michigan side of the lake. Those who weren't cheering applauded in awe.

In slow motion, the platform she stood upon lowered beneath the stage. As the last of the string section began to fade, the band director wiped tears from his eyes and turned, smiling at the audience. Stage hands had to raise the platform again, so Coco could take a bow as the applause wore on, something nobody had planned on. The applause still didn't fade until she was gone again, and even then, Mayor Kelly had to hold his palms out to quiet the crowd.

Mac suddenly felt insulted. Having Mayor Ed Kelly quieting Coco's applause was sacrilege as far as he was concerned. There was nothing Kelly could say that would ever measure up to the sound Mac had just heard. Coco's music shared some universal kind of truth, while Kelly's entire political platform was based on "not being a reformer." He was a liar and the next best thing to a racketeer.

Somebody in the city office must have felt the same way, because before the applause had died Kelly muttered something into the microphone, and Don McNeill, host of the local NBC Blue Network's Breakfast show took the platform.

"Good Evening, Century of Progress! Ladies and Gentlemen! And welcome to the Annual Mayor's Medal Ceremony, where our own outstanding citizens and those of our sister cities across the world are honored for their service to The City of Chicago." The emcee waved an arm presenting the honorees gathered around a table behind him. Decorative desk lamps lighted the silhouettes, the green lamp shades flashing on them to reveal the faces of the winners one at a time.

Mac scanned the table. Two Boy Scouts, two firemen, one uniformed policeman, a real estate broker disguised as a city planner, and two men in European-cut tuxes and tails already wearing medals of some sort, probably the reason for the mention of sister cities. One seat at the end of the table remained empty.

Mac turned to say something to Crankshaft, but his friend was already gone. Scanning the crowd, Mac could see the ace mechanic sneaking around the orchestra pit, making his way backstage to meet Coco. Mac sighed. He'd have to wait to congratulate his favorite torch singer. Three was still a crowd.

The two Boy Scouts were awarded medals for collecting door-to-door donations for the poor. It took guts to go into some of these neighborhoods asking for dough when so many people were already broke, Mac thought, *especially in short pants.* He watched the kids' families clap, thought about sneaking off to the Midway and coming back. He was getting tired of being the fifth wheel. Maybe if he played his cards right, he could see what Sally Rand was doing for dinner.

He started to get up, and an attractive woman with the Boy Scout's cheering section gave him a dirty look. If it had been a man he'd have stood up and left. But she was an attractive woman. Mac sat back down and gave her his best pleasant smile. She turned as if offended, but Mac saw her steal another glance, from the corner of her eye, of course, all the while pretending not to.

Maybe he wouldn't go to the Midway after all.

The city planner got his medal for some construction being done. Mac made a mental note to check up on that. Between the mayor, his buddies, and the mob, the concrete on that project would probably be substandard and brittle by next week.

Then he realized he was thinking about cleaning up the city, again. Why did he do that? He was born here and made a pretty good living playing both ends against the middle. The Bagman seemed to be keeping his neighborhood pretty clean. Isn't that what he'd heard all his life? Keep your side of the street clean.

Problem was Chicago had a lot of streets, and pretty soon you begin to notice the blood flowing in the gutter from the next block. And it made Mac angry. He'd have to have a word with the mayor later.

Meanwhile, there were always people to watch. Reporters taking notes and snapping pictures in the crowd. The men in evening wear looking uncomfortable in the summer heat. Men in suits with jackets slung over their shoulders, smoking cigars, leaning back in their seats with their legs crossed. The ones with wives and girlfriends getting elbowed to straighten up and look proper.

Mac pulled a cigarette out of his coat, lit it, and leaned back in his chair a moment, then slowly turned sideways. There were three large boats on the lake directly across from the auditorium. A newsreel team stood on the grass to the side, commemorating the event. A photographer with his camera on a tripod stood opposite, his head under its black hood, his arm held halfway out, thumb striking a handheld control. Kids ran playing in the sand on the beach just outside the fence.

The fireman got his award. The uniform cop got his. Mac kept staring at the brown haired woman with the Boy Scout. Mayor Kelly took the microphone. Mac ignored him for as long as he could, but part of the mayor's condescension finally leaked through.

"… As we've organized this World's Fair, Chicago has made friends from all over the world. But one of our greatest friends has been Bucharest, Romania, who have not only shared their wonderful culture with us, but also their beautiful architecture which still inspires even Chicagoans! And so it is my pleasure to present this medal from, not just me, but the City of Chicago and our Century of Progress. Ladies and gentleman, The Romanian ambassador, Vornic Bogdad Daciana!"

The crowd applauded politely. One of the gentlemen in European-cut tuxedoes stood up, straightened his gray striped pants, and strode to the podium.

"Ladies and gentleman of Chicago and the world!" he said, with only the trace of an accent. The crowd applauded some more.

Mac took a second look. The ambassador was sweating. Sure it was hot, but he was twitchy, seemed to be glancing from left to right like something was going to pounce on him.

Or maybe he was just a nervous speaker, Mac thought, as the ambassador shuffled the papers in front of him looking lost. The ambassador mumbled something and glanced back toward the mayor's seat. Then he turned back to the microphone. There was a strange, high pitched, whooping sound feeding back from the microphone. It grew higher and thinned out.

"I had a very…specially prepared, how you say…speech, my friends, but it seems to have been misplaced." He rifled through the papers on the podium once more, stared out at the crowd.

Definitely a nervous speaker, Mac thought as the ambassador stood there open mouthed. Then the Romanian just kept standing there, frozen. Without warning, he began shaking in seizures, as a string of drool dropped from his lips and wound its way down to the podium. Then his back stiffened, like he'd been electrified. He shook more violently.

And began to rise in the air.

High-pitched feedback wailed from the microphone, and the crowd covered their ears. The ambassador hung a foot above the stage with his arms extended, his entire body vibrating. His eyes swelled and pleaded, he screamed in broken pulses like an animal at bay.

Suddenly, the feedback stopped. The ambassador remained hanging in the air, his jaw clenched, his eyes wedged shut. There was a moment of silence, the crowd hushed.

And the ambassador exploded.

Or more like, he just popped. A red mist filled the air, but the ambassador's suit just hung there a moment, suddenly colored red-black with the same blood as the mist, before it dropped to the ground in a moist wad.

A family in the front row screamed as Mac vaulted the stairs at the edge of the orchestra pit and hopped onstage. The uniformed policeman stood over the ambassador's clothes with his gun out, looking for an assailant.

Unfortunately, all that gun waving wasn't helping the confusion. The front row stood looking befuddled, but people were starting to panic and when they got home, some of those men in tuxes were going to have to explain why they pushed the family out of the way trying to escape. Reporters ran both towards the stage and away from it. The kids on the beach peeked through the fence wondering what the commotion was about. The newsreel crew kept filming, but the photographer with the tripod was breaking down his equipment fast.

Fine, thought Mac, *less people, less innocent bystanders. If they don't kill themselves first.*

The cop pointed the gun at Mac.

Mac raised his hands, and held out his ticket. "Whoa there, cowboy! You're spooking the audience!"

The young policeman caught himself, seemed to hold his breath and then exhale. He gave Mac a nod, and lowered the gun. "You see anything?"

"Nothing. He just started shaking and popped. I didn't even hear a cap explode."

The cop looked down at the puddle of blood and fabric. Mac began to back away. He needed a look backstage, whatever happened could have been rigged there. He backed into somebody behind him at the exact same time he recognized the nameplate sitting at the vacant spot at the awards table.

Lieutenant Detective Jacob Costanovitch, Chicago Police. The same Detective Costanovitch The Bagman had called at four this morning to let him know the First State Bank of Illinois was being robbed.

Backing around the detective, Mac pulled his hat down low, trying to block his face with his arm so he couldn't be recognized. A canned ham of a hand gripped his bicep and pulled it out of the way. There was a glint of recognition in the detective's eyes as he held onto McCullough's arm.

Mac had been introduced to the detective only once; but twice he had held him at gunpoint as The Bagman. Mac tilted his head and stared at the puddle that had been the Romanian ambassador, then gave the detective a purposely clueless look.

"Mac McCullough, right? Mac's Tobacco?" Costanovitch let go of his arm. The detective recognized Mac from his cigar store; the one he had promised himself would never be just a front but had become just that.

Mac exhaled, and realized he'd been holding his breath. Costanovitch was not only smart, but even worse he was an honest cop. All things considered, it would be better if Mac stayed off the investigator's radar completely. On the other hand, it occurred to him this might be his only chance to look at the scene. He idled behind Costanovitch, looking almost as if the detective had requested his presence.

Costanovitch approached the podium, stepping over the pile of bloody tuxedo. Mac grabbed the pages of the ambassador's speech, now pink with Romanian blood, off the top of the podium.

"Ladies and gentleman! Please do not be alarmed!" Costanovitch said, in a controlled voice over the microphone. "Please, people of Chicago! There's no need for panic. It's all part of the show!"

The hush of fear gave way to mumbles in the crowd.

"All part of an act." The detective dug deeper.

Somebody in the crowd whooped. Somebody else tried to chuckle. A golf-clap started and stumbled through the audience. Seeing Mayor Kelly behind him, Detective Costanovitch grabbed him by the wrist. To an onlooker it might have looked like the detective was shaking his hand, but to the mayor it was obvious; the detective had him in his grip. He shoved Kelly toward the podium.

"Tell 'em the ambassador's a magician. Tell 'em it's part of a Ripley's Believe It or Not gag…tell 'em anything…but do not let them know what happened. Get it, Mayor?"

From the look on Kelly's face it was obvious he didn't, but it was also obvious he had no choice.

"Yes, ladies and gentleman, as you well know, our Bohemian friends are steeped not only in a history of spiritual mystery, but downright magic…" Kelly ad libbed. "In fact, not only will we be giving out free passes for rides, but the first fifty attendees to line up outside the band shell gate will receive free passes to the Ripley's Believe It Or Not exhibition!"

Mac did a double take, amazed at how quickly Kelly had launched into his velvet voiced, political demeanor. Then he waved Detective Costanovitch over with the pink copies of the ambassador's speech. "I don't know what it means, but I'm betting you'd like a look at this."

It was a ransom note, placed on the podium instead of the ambassador's speech, perhaps in the hope that he would read it aloud.

✹ ✹ ✹

Chicago and the World,

I will kill one man, woman, or child at the fair every hour, until I receive one-million dollars. Don't try to evacuate the park. I have men stationed at the exits. If people should begin leaving in large numbers, I'll cut them down by the thousand (into even smaller pieces than the ambassador).

If you agree to the terms simply have NBC broadcaster, Don McNeil use the phrase 'zeitgeist resonates with the people.' If you do not...you will be next.

From the lamb of the sister city,
To the Hall on the Great Explorer,
The sky's the limit for State and Fed,
Pay Resonance, or you're all dead.

--Resonance

Detective Costanovitch scratched the quote about zeitgeist onto a pad of paper, and handed it to Don McNeil onstage. The radio announcer rushed to the booth to get the quote on the air immediately.

It was obvious the Romanian Ambassador had been the *"lamb of the sister city."* Mac gave the poem some thought, without thinking about it too much. When he'd finished reading it, he backed toward the stage door, hoping Costanivitch wouldn't notice. Whatever had killed the ambassador wasn't readily visible here. Turning on the steps, he spotted Crankshaft and Coco Blue.

"You guys OK?"

"Fine," Coco said, with a wink. She was trying to act chipper, wrapped in a white robe and fanning herself with the feathers on her headpiece, but there was still a tear on her cheek. Visibly disturbed, the torch singer managed to banter. "But we've got to stop meeting like this, Mac."

"You mean in stupid situations, or just backstage after murders?" Crankshaft said.

"I think she means with you around, Crank." Mac looked at a drop of blood leaking through the floorboards above them. "See anything else?"

"Nothing," Crankshaft said, waving an arm. "And the place is wide open. I didn't see anybody so much as throw a switch."

"Huh, I wonder if any of the photographers might have gotten a picture of..." Mac eyes went wide. He slammed the heel of his fist into his palm. "The photographer, Crank!"

"But it could take weeks to get all the pictures people took…"

"No, Crank, *the* photographer. There was a guy with a tripod out there, not part of the newsreel crew, and he was wearing an old-world tuxedo with striped pants just like the ambassador!"

The band upstairs launched into a version of The Stars and Stripes Forever in an effort to keep the crowd from panicking.

Just like on the Titanic, Mac thought, as he jettisoned himself back up the stairs, pinballing through the crew still milling on the steps. A foreign looking tuxedo wasn't much of a clue, but it was the one thing that stood out at the scene of the crime. And it was a lot easier to believe the ambassador had enemies on foreign soil, than it was to believe he just spontaneously…

Popped. That was the only word for it.

The big man raced past the crowd lined up for free tickets. To his right sat the lake, and a circular walkway back to the entrance. To his left half the fairgrounds. Mac figured if this guy was asking for a ransom he wasn't leaving. Feeling for the mask in his pocket, he turned into a wave of summer straw hats and the screams of a thousand children. Before Mac realized it, he was broken field running. But, to a man who'd spent half his life committing crimes it just seemed like running. And he was good at it.

Sliding around small packs, he worked his way through the crowd, twisting when blocked, only to slink around another human obstacle without having to break stride. It may not have been artful dodging, but it was agile.

Mac kept his peripheral vision on the beach and scanned the shows on the other side as he ran past. The Horticultural exhibit at the far corner had a line; if his quarry had gotten that far he probably wasn't hidden in the bushes. Screams of children emanated from the Enchanted Island next to it.

Enchanted Island was supposed to be a kiddy ride, a fantasy land just for children; a full-grown photographer would stand out like a hernia at a body-building competition there. Mac glanced at some fairy-tale statues in front as he loped past the island, and wondered for the thousandth time why Cinderella's glass slipper hadn't turned back into old boots at midnight.

He twisted around two more straw boaters and a parasol, just in time to see a tripod folded under the arm of a man walking the other way. He lost the man behind a balloon vendor, then caught glimpse of a gray striped pant cuff as it disappeared behind the door to the Electrical Group building, where the crowd would be lined up inside.

Mac turned immediately and cut across the lawn to cut the distance between him and the suspect. The Criminal Detective yanked the door open, took two steps and stopped.

To his right, he saw the photographer carrying a tripod under the same arm he used to grasp the large box camera. The shutterbug's uneven strides made him stand out all the more as he tried to disappear down the hallway.

Then, without warning, a man in a navy blazer blocked the path between Mac and his quarry. Standing in the center of the floor, he pointed something in his hand at Mac.

A magic wand.

Chapter Five
THE BAGMAN
BREAKS OUT

It was a shiny black rod, with the end of it lit up like a Roman candle.

Having just seen the ambassador of Romania turned into a hamburger frappé, Mac hit the dirt, or more precisely, the tile floor.

Glancing up at the man with the wand, Mac rolled across the floor and came up behind a table with his hand on his gun. As his view crossed the tabletop, a light bulb on it erupted into brilliance. Blinded, The Bagman ducked beneath the table covering his eyes, and the crowd began to applaud.

Mac heard some children giggle. A woman milling about in the crowd sneered and made a comment about "some people." He rubbed his eyes, and the brightness under the lids eventually blotted till he only saw spots.

Above him loomed a large, well groomed man with a pencil thin mustache. He wore gray slacks and a blue blazer with the General Electric Lighting Corporation's logo on it.

Mac groaned and remembered one of the big exhibits at the Electrical Group was "wireless incandescent lighting." They'd turned it into a magic act, and he'd stepped right into the middle of it.

The G.E. rep smiled pleasantly and bowed toward Mac as if he were part of the act, then waved the wand toward a standing parlor lamp down the same curved hall the mysterious photographer ran down.

Mac sprung from the floor as another small mob swarmed it. The sudden influx of fairgoers hardly noticed him, as they marveled at their bags of popcorn, popped by invisible radioactive microwaves. Mac balanced his way through the crowd, leaning side to side, and trying to not to knock anybody's popcorn out of their hand. He took the turn down the hall leaning at a forty-five degree angle. The onlookers laughed, thinking he was part of the act, chasing down the lights as they switched on and off.

Mac didn't know what he was after. But he knew it was bad.

As big as it was, the shutterbug hadn't dropped the camera case. There was something in there. The photographer continued moving away from the press tent; too hurried to be a typical fairgoer. Too fast to be just another Midway carnie.

Mac didn't like anybody getting away from him. As far as he was concerned, he'd invented the getaway and what he really didn't like was he hadn't even seen the photographers face.

Yet.

The man with the camera cleared the hall and trotted across the large open space of the Social Science exhibit, where he opened a door marked "Employees Only."

Mac hit the floor spinning on one foot, just in time to see the man's back going through the door behind him. Still turning, he spotted another employee entrance just to his left. With any luck, he could pull the same trick he'd used entering the Electrical Building. If he couldn't head off the shutterbug at the pass, he might still meet him at its edge.

Mac's shoulder hit the exit door, and his hand reached for the disguise in his pocket. A menacing, broad-shouldered figure with a mask and a revolver came out the other side.

The maintenance hallway ran parallel to the wall behind the exhibit, the only exit behind the scenes being a hallway between the doors both men had used. In other words, the photographer had to double back.

Mac's quarry stopped in front of a broom closet, as if he sensed something.

A body block bounced him off the wall. The shutterbug collapsed, and the camera hit the ground tumbling. The lensman jumped to his feet, fists raised. Turning quickly, he froze when he realized he was looking down the barrel of a .45. The two blue eyes above the sights were like ice.

"Funny thing about social science," the masked man said, ratcheting the gun's hammer back, "it says crime has a culture all its own."

The photographer gasped for air, and Mac got a look at his face. He was an average looking guy except for the goatee: brown hair, brown eyes, medium complexion, medium everything. Without the trimmed beard he could have been anybody. The man's fists opened, and he held them above his head.

"Take whatever you want, mister. Please, I don't want any trouble."

"Nice act, 'Barrymore'. But what I want is a look at that camera." The Bagman's left hand reached in the photographer's jacket and patted his waist searching for a gun. Then he pulled the shutterbug's wallet out of his dinner jacket, and shoved the photographer face first into the wall. Rifling through the wallet, Mac found $133 in bills and a business card. No names or business numbers were listed on the card, only one initial, "R", and a picture of a megaphone speaker with tentacles spreading ominously from the inside of it. Mac stuck the card in his pocket.

The camera lay face down at an angle, apparently resting on its lens. The Bagman stepped backward, carefully, and, with the gun still aimed at the lensman, prodded at the cloth curtain behind the camera with his other hand. He swept the fabric over the top of camera exposing…

Nothing.

It wasn't even a camera. It was an empty wooden box painted black. Even the lens that kept it from sitting level on the floor wasn't real. The opening in front of the camera was simply a hollow wooden tube.

No evidence, just the smell. Something rotten.

The Bagman spun the shutterbug back around, and shoved him toward the broom closet, yanking the door open, and stepping inside with his prey.

"What's the scam, Mister R? Because I'm guessing there's not a lot of profit in pretending to take pictures."

"This is none of your business," the faux photographer said. "Leave me alone, or you'll be forced to pay."

A tingle ran up the back of Mac's neck. The guy hadn't even pretended to make up an excuse. *A whole ocean of rotten.* He grappled the lensman by the hair and slammed his head into the wall.

"You don't get it, do ya, snappy? I want my cut!"

"You're in my world. Over your head."

Mac slammed the photographer's head into the back of the closet. "Ask around. You steal in Chicago, The Bagman gets his cut." It was all bluster, but it usually worked. You want to deal with a mobster, *be* a mobster.

Mac stepped back. "Take off your belt and shoelaces. You may be tied up for awhile."

The photographer began to laugh, but there was nothing heartwarming about it. The laughter transformed to a bone-chilling cackle; the call of a mythical bird of prey as it cracked the barrier between sanity and madness. The prisoner didn't even bother to reach for his belt, much less his shoelaces. Instead he raised the heel of his foot and kicked the wall behind him twice fast, then once.

The back of the closet wall opened up, and gun barrels peered out of the darkness on the other side. One of the barrels was backed by a round drum. The cartridge for a Thompson Sub-machinegun.

The masked man jumped sideways, and the wall behind him erupted into a hundred bullet holes.

Yup, definitely something fishy here, Mac thought, careening off the wall and exploding around a corner as the bullets stitched their way behind him.

One of the ceiling lights above him exploded. He turned right, headed back toward the Electrical Group, when he remembered the crowd of innocent bystanders. A bullet whizzed by, tearing at his sleeve. The Bagman pitched in the other direction.

"Kill him!" the photographer screamed.

Three bullets cut into the wall next to The Bagman's head. That's when

Mac realized he hadn't heard any gunshots. He bounded for the only other exit available, the hall to the Horticultural Exhibit. Bullets pounded the door as it shut behind him.

He sprinted for the exit on the other side of the room. Mac knew if he could reach the Horticulture Exhibit there might be fewer people, and some plants to hide behind. He cleared the next door as leaden death stitched a burst of fire from the other side, only to realize he'd taken a wrong turn somewhere.

He locked the door behind him, as if that would do any good. He'd missed Horticulture completely and stepped into something else. Another hallway, almost like a gymnasium with hardwood floors.

Hurtling down the corridor, The Bagman glimpsed another Janitor's closet. Only this one was already open, and not full of gunmen. His eyes swam over the cleaning supplies. One of his hands whisked a gallon jug of liquid off the floor. There was a mop bucket on wheels by the far door.

His wrong turn may have slowed his pursuers, but he could hear the clamor of footsteps and threats coming up behind him, even if he couldn't hear the shots.

The Bagman opened one of the jugs and took a whiff. Even through the leather facemask, the smell almost knocked him out. He put that jug to the side and holstered his gun, then pulled a separate glass jug from the closet floor and hurled it toward the door behind him.

The glass jug shattered, and the smell of bleach began to waft through the air. Mac pulled out two more jugs and did the same, but threw the bottles closer hoping to spread the liquid out on the floor.

He didn't have time. Running for the opposite exit, he grabbed the jug of fluid he'd set to the side. Something outside went "*whut!*", and a bullet ripped through the door, splintering the floorboards. *Whut!* again, and the door handle popped across the room. Still holding the jug of fluid, Mac grabbed the bucket with his right hand as he spun through the exit, the double doors swaying behind him.

Doing an odd little dance, he swung the bucket around in front of him and emptied the gallon jug into it. Hesitating a moment, he turned his head from the smell and considered the action he was about to take. A bullet ripped through the wall and made his mind up for him.

Pouring the last of the contents of the gallon jug into the bucket, Mac faced the two scarred, wire-reinforced windows on the doors again. He could barely see the men coming at him.

They couldn't see him at all.

Mac put his heel against the side of the bucket and kicked it through the door.

"Look out!" one of the mobsters yelled, dodging to the side as the bucket skittered across the hardwood and tipped over in front him. The contents spilled across the floor.

""Look out for what," said one of the gunmen, kicking the empty container. "It's a bucket full of floor cleaner." Chuckling to himself, the gangster turned, took two steps, and collapsed to the floor unconscious.

The man next to him fell backwards. Two men behind him coughed, and fell over. The last two gangsters yanked the door open and entered the room then, reeling and coughing, made their way slowly back out the door they'd come in. One of them collapsed on the other side.

"Bleach and ammonia equals chlorine gas, guys," Mac said to himself. "There's a reason they outlawed it in the war."

He tore his mask off and headed in the other direction.

Mac hadn't wanted to use the lethal mixture on the rank-and-file goons, but he hadn't wanted to draw attention by firing his gun, either. Speaking of which, how were those guys firing guns that didn't go *bang*? Part of him wanted to go back and look at their hardware, but between waiting for the gas to disperse and the crowd, he couldn't risk being seen around two violent scenes in the same day.

Mac pulled the brim of his hat down, stuck his hands in his pockets, and shuffled out of the Botanical exhibit. The sun had set, but the torches and tiny lights reflecting off the lagoon and illuminating the displays gave it a feeling of never-ending twilight. Back on the sidewalk, he took a look at a display map of the Fairgrounds and found the symbol for "You are here."

Something hit him in the rear end. Mac turned, and a boy around seven years old was standing behind him.

"Oh, sorry about that, sir." The boy wore dilapidated knickers, no socks, and next to his suspenders, obviously from some European country, hung a World's Fair Employee badge.

"It's all right, kid," Mac said. Looking back at the map, he noted the locations of several other exhibits and checked his watch. For a moment the boy's suspenders crossed his mind. That's when he reached for his hip pocket and realized the innocent looking kid had just stolen his wallet.

"Why you stinkin' little Gypsy…"

Mac turned and saw the two, tiny, bare calves speeding in the other direction. The kid, dark hair falling in his eyes, even turned his head and smiled at Mac. McCullough growled as he tried to swim upstream through a throng of people, but the crowd was just too thick.

Something from behind him clasped his bicep. Mac jumped in surprise.

It was Coco. She'd changed out of her stage gear and was wearing a rose-colored sweater dress that might have looked more conservative on a woman with fewer curves.

"Mac McCullough, are you alright?" Even her spoken voice was soothing.

"Bleach and ammonia equals chlorine gas, guys."

"Don't ask." Mac was still shocked over his unexpected use of chlorine gas to defend himself. He wasn't the type who enjoyed killing people, and he certainly didn't want to talk about the fact that he might have just ended five men's lives. "Listen, Coco, where's…?"

"Right here," Crankshaft said, behind him. Nobody had ever been able to sneak up on Mac except for the big man's closest friends. The ace mechanic seemed to take a perverse pleasure in it sometimes.

Mac looked over his shoulder. The ragged little Gypsy had stopped running and stood still at the edge of the path. The boy grinned, motioning with his finger for Mac to follow, taunting him. Mac looked at his watch again. Despite the throng of the crowd, he could feel the second hand ticking.

Ten minutes to a killing.

"Now's not the time, Crank," Mac said, "This Resonance guy's got a small army of muscle and they're armed for bear with guns that go *pffft* instead of *bang*. I caught up with the photographer, and I'd just had time to find out his camera was a fake when the goons started shooting."

"Guns that go *pffft*?"

"Automatics and some kind of weird Tommy gun with extra chambers on the barrel."

"You think they used some kind of special bullet on the ambassador?"

"Don't know. They were shooting real ones at me." Mac still didn't mention that he might have killed half a dozen men.

"Can you do me a favor, Crank?"

Crankshaft's brows folded in concern. "Not till I know what it is."

"Don't worry. I just need to see if you can find Hunts Helms. I'm willing to bet he's at the Old Heidelberg Inn instead of the Press Club. Maybe he can give us the lowdown on our cops and robbers."

Hunts Helms was a reporter for the city of Chicago. A semi-reformed confidence man from Mac's old days, Hunts had created the position himself. He called it public relations, but he was more like a promotional agent than a reporter.

"Hunts was backstage at the medal ceremony," Crankshaft said, "trying to get the big scoop right after you ran off. He's at the Heidelberg. The cops are still trying to decipher that note, but after '*From the lambs of the sister city*,' comes the sentence "*to the Hall on the Great Explorer.* So it's got to be Admiral Byrd's "City of New York," the ship from his Arctic expedition in the lagoon, right?"

"Could be, but take a look at that map, Crank. The Hall of Science is on Leif Erickson Drive; a hall *on* a great explorer. And, that's the direction the shutterbug was headed when I stopped him."

"I'll see if I can find a phone somewhere near, set up some kind of communication with Hunts. Then I'll see you there."

"I'm not asking you to do that, Crank," Mac said. He winked at Coco. "Sure you're not trying to impress the girl?"

"It's not about that."

Coco's eyes narrowed at Crankshaft.

"It's not *just* about that," Crankshaft said. "If all hell breaks loose, I want to know which way we run."

"Bring a gun." The bagman turned vigilante looked serious for once.

Crankshaft looked up at the sky and sighed. Unlike Mac, he didn't go everywhere with a shoulder holster on.

Mac added, "Try to find a phone near the Midway. There's a thief on the fair's payroll I want to catch, too."

Crankshaft's brows furrowed as he imagined The Bagman capturing the hucksters in front of the Freak Show.

"Sorry, Coco," Mac said, tipping his hat. "Gotta blow."

Coco giggled. Mac turned with a brisk stride north and sprinted down the path toward the Hall of Science.

"'Gotta blow?'" Crankshaft asked, "You find that appealing?"

They exhaled in a half effort to chuckle that seemed to force the last vestige of humor from them.

"Something seemed to be bothering Mac," Coco said. "I don't know what he's dealing with, but I hope he's the man for it."

Crankshaft tilted his head forward and then came up with a half smile. "Y'know, in a situation where nobody knows what's going on, he's the first one I'd trust."

They looked into each other's eyes with a mixture of fear and hope, and sped up their step.

Chapter Six
THE TELETRACTOR

Nine minutes till the next death.

The youthful pickpocket just happened to be on the same path Mac hurried down toward the Hall of Science. But for every step Mac took, the tiny pickpocket took two. It took all of the big man's willpower not to start chasing him, but eventually he lost the kid in the crowd. Mac turned off the pathway and cut across the grounds to face the Hall of Science. It was the first time he'd seen the building outside of a newspaper photo.

The black and white pictures hadn't done it justice. The Hall of Science's exterior was covered in violent shades of orange, blue, red and white. And that was without all the lights. Problem was, the building covered eight acres. The guidebook alone was a hundred-and-eighty-four pages, and Mac didn't know where to start.

He looked around for some sort of sign and saw nothing. Closing his eyes, he stood like a boulder in a stream as the crowd washed around him. Instinct pulled him to the right, towards the main hall.

Turning, he saw the Gypsy boy by the entrance still motioning with his finger for Mac to catch him. Mac broke into a sprint, and the kid hightailed it inside. Mac bolted through the door to the main hall, all the while trying not to pay attention to the annoying little pickpocket; he may have wanted to wring the kid's neck, but The Bagman's strange sense of duty was more important.

Inside, Mac stopped and stared. The place looked like a toy store for adults. The main hall itself was enormous, and there seemed to be at least twenty different hallways leading to other scientific wonders. Behind that, of course, were even more hallways representing countless other countries across the globe.

Both Jean Piccard's balloon gondola, scheduled for a record-breaking flight next month, and a gigantic bathysphere hung from the ceiling, blocking Mac's view to the left. To the right a gigantic display of the Periodic Table of Elements stood next to rubber and electro-chemistry exhibits. It would've helped if Mac knew what had killed the ambassador to begin with. At least then he'd have a clue as to which way to go.

His head pivoting, Mac spotted a sign at the far end of the hall by the table of elements. *Medical Section.* Seemed like a better bet than Geology. Mac raced past an animatronic "growing twig," spotted a fire-alarm on the farm wall, and found himself strangely grateful for the Chicago fire. Want some of the toughest fire regulations anywhere? Burn the city down and wait about forty years.

He didn't bother using the tiny hammer attached to the alarm to break the glass, but shoved his elbow through it on the run and yanked on the handle. What the hell, the suit was already full of holes.

Bells roared in a deafening clang. People in the crowd started, and then headed for the doors, guards guiding them. Mac slid around the corner on the balls of his feet, past a display for the cell and into embryology. A security guard, hand on holster, approached him. It probably didn't help that Mac rolled his eyes when he was forced to stop.

"Fire Alarm! Everybody out of the hall!" The guard gave him a stern look.

Mac almost punched him out, then remembered he didn't have his mask on.

"It's all right, Police business," he said, and reached for his wallet, where he kept a five-pointed star from the Tom Mix Fan Club. Even if he'd had it, he wouldn't have had time to use it.

The security guard almost closed one eye peering inside his jacket. He might have seen the gun. "Cop, eh? You don't look like no cop."

Not giving the watchman time to think, Mac continued to reach for his wallet as if he were about to pull out the biggest badge since Wyatt Earp. He pointed in the other direction, and yelled, "Look out! The Genetics Exhibit!"

The security guard's glance followed Mac's finger, and the fist behind McCullough's back shot up from the floor in a perfect uppercut. A one punch knockout. Mac didn't have time to brag about it.

All about him was confusion. Alarm bells clanging, people panicking. Meanwhile, Mac was trying to locate an unknown killing machine in a building the size of a ranch.

He heard an unending scream coming from up the hallway. And the beginning of a *whiz-bang*. That same loud whistle he'd heard before the Romanian ambassador had exploded at the Mayor's Medal Ceremony. It was coming from just up the hall, the same place as the scream.

Passing a display of Comparative Anatomy, Mac saw a woman hooked up to a machine that resembled a treadmill just beyond it. The woman stood, screaming, hitting and pushing at an odd electric box on a stand, attached to her abdomen. The woman shook so fast she began to blur, but Mac still recognized her. The pretty lady who had been sitting with the Boy Scout's family at the Mayor's Medal presentation. The one Mac had wanted to ask out.

He thought about the empty camera box, and realized this one wasn't empty.

Drawing his revolver, he fired at the machine. The first bullet seemed to ricochet off the top, though it was hard to tell in all the confusion. Mac emptied his gun at it. Sparks and smoke wheezed from the machine's vents, as the black finish popped off in chunks revealing the steel beneath.

The high pitched drone began to weaken and subside. The woman locked to the machine peeled off and collapsed to the floor, her skin speckled red and blue from broken blood vessels and internal bleeding. Mac reloaded his gun, cursing the entire time.

A sign above the machine read "The Teletractor: Hearing for the Deaf."

And death for whoever's hooked up to the thing, Mac thought. He didn't have time to read the captions below the machine to find out what it was; the footsteps of a small group echoed behind him, most likely cops or security.

He glanced up from the shattered body of the Teletractor's victim, wondering if she'd been picked at random. It seemed highly likely. The whole thing could've been rigged up ahead of time, and all the killer photographer would have to do is wait for a victim, anybody. To whoever was pulling the strings it didn't matter.

Mac growled and, instead of making a break for the stairs, began scaling the shelves on the wall next to the now-shattered and cracked Dresden Dolls displaying human anatomy. He had to lean over the shelves as he climbed, in order not to pull them off the wall, and with every step upward a ceramic person or some human organ fell on the floor and shattered. It didn't seem to bother him at all as he climbed on up to the next one, eventually reaching the ledge on the second floor. He grabbed one of the rungs on the railing and swung himself over, peeking out just in time to see three security guards looking down and tsk-tsking over the dead body.

There was no way to reach the crawlspace behind the Teletractor from above, and absolutely no way to get a look at the machine itself. Mac headed down the hall toward micro-biology where he saw a sign that said "Death Ray."

"*If it was only that simple,* he thought. But the death ray on display only killed bacteria. He took the rear stairs back down and managed to get back outside without being spotted.

Back in the fresh air, he pressed his fists to his eyes, massaging the sockets as he stood separate from the world for a moment. He looked at his watch. Fifty-three minutes till the next murder.

Fifty-three minutes to once again search an entire four-hundred acres, over twenty-five city blocks. Four hours and he might have stood a chance.

Problem was, he was already tired. He hadn't gotten much sleep and the marathon hadn't even started. He needed a way to stop this thing, and fast.

Mac pushed his hair under his hat and shoved it back down on his head, before turning toward the Midway. Two-hundred yards away the Gypsy boy in suspenders stood in front of the Edward's Rancho exhibit, just outside the Midway gate, his finger crooked in the universal signal for "come here."

Mac's chest inflated and the rest of his body seemed to flex and contract around it. When he raised his face, it was bright red. His eyebrows came down in what should have been the universal symbol for evil, and a devilish smile formed at the edges of his lips. He leaned forward like a bull about to charge.

Yet the Gypsy kid never stopped smiling.

Something grabbed Mac by the arm. Without looking the ex-mobster tried to brush the grip off, and another hand grabbed the brush off. Both hands belonged to Crankshaft.

The ace mechanic had traded his summer blazer for a cotton windbreaker with an Army Colt Automatic in the pocket. "Any luck?"

"Yeah, all bad," Mac said. "What about you?"

Crankshaft pointed behind Mac, at a telephone booth in front of the Hall of Science, and handed him a piece of paper with two phone numbers written on it.

"Top number is that phone, bottom is the Heidelberg Inn," he said. "I figure we stick to those two, we're more likely to stay in touch."

"Great, but we don't even know where this guy's going next. And Crank, I've got a feeling he *wants* to kill a lot more people. He's just toying with us." Mac sunk his chin in his palm and shrugged. "What about the press room? Shouldn't we link up with each other there? At least then we'd know what's going on."

"Cops aren't telling the press a thing, except about how they decided to give away free tickets to Ripley's Believe It or Not."

Mac started to say he didn't believe it. Crankshaft didn't let him.

"Nobody's saying anything at the fairground police station either, but I did happen to see Detective Costanovitch headed over to the Old Heidelberg Inn with some other law-and-order types. Probably why our reporter friend, Hunts, frequents the place."

"Hunts frequents the place because it's a bar. Do me a favor, would ya? Call over there and have him meet us at the Medical Science exhibits." Mac's finger probed at the hole in his lapel. "And tell him to bring some coffee."

"I don't think you're allowed to take drinks out of The Heidelberg," Crankshaft said, matter-of-factly.

Mac's eyes rolled out from under a serious brow, and came back down with a tilt of the head that asked if Crank was serious.

Crankshaft sighed. Mac's crowd practically went out of their way to break the rules. The ace mechanic tilted his head toward a small group of uniformed policemen crossing the lawn toward the Hall of Science.

"See you there in ten."

Mac kept his back turned so his face wouldn't be seen, letting the policemen pass as Crankshaft walked in the same direction. The big man took a couple of steps toward the Midway, looked up, didn't see the junior pickpocket, turned around and took a couple of steps toward the map displayed on the path. He stopped halfway, closed his eyes again and shook his head, wondering what he was up against.

And what the hell was a Teletractor, anyway?

"It's a machine that allows deaf people to 'feel' the sound of another person's voice," Crankshaft said, describing the Teletractor. "They press it against their diaphragm and 'hear' the vibration of a spoken word."

Crankshaft and Mac were standing by the ledge directly above the scene of the crime, where Mac had climbed to avoid the police only minutes before. Behind them sat Coco and Hunts Helms, next to a beer cart loaded with sandwiches that Hunts had rolled in. Hunts hadn't volunteered to say where he got it, and nobody had bothered to ask. The four of them watched as policemen combed the area around the corpse for clues.

"The general public has been lining up for Teletractor demonstrations for days now." Crankshaft paused and sipped his drink. "This 'Resonance' character just had to wait. Somebody hits the demo button, signs his own death warrant."

"I'm surprised some of our city fathers haven't figured out a way to rig up something like that in a voting booth," Hunts said.

"Probably have." Crankshaft stared at his cup. "Just realized they'd kill the goose that laid the golden egg."

"Yeah, that's the problem with graft," Hunts said. "Take the honest people out, and it kills all the profit."

Mac's eyes narrowed. Normally he'd be the first to joke in a tough situation, but he was thinking about the woman he'd been attracted to at the Mayor's Medal Ceremony. A woman who had been murdered seemingly at random, leaving the rest of the Boy Scout's family behind.

Hunts shoved a cigarette in his mouth and lighted it. "You OK, Mac?"

Mac put his coffee down and began pacing, pretending to listen to the conversation, and watching the police collect clues. "Yeah...Yeah, I'm fine."

Hunts shrugged his shoulders and sighed. Mac wrapped a hand around the lower part of his face and massaged his jaw.

"He's doing it with sound," he muttered under his breath.

"What?" Crankshaft had been staring blankly out the window.

"Sound. Maybe this guy's some sort of sonic genius. I mean, he killed that lady with sound, or vibration, whatever." Mac pointed at the corpse below. "Looks like he killed the ambassador the same way and what about the guns that didn't go bang?"

"Doesn't take a genius to make one of those," Crankshaft said. "I saw the detective down there showing one of the guns to his buddies. That chamber on the barrel is called a silencer except it should be called a baffle, or a muffler, because nobody's been able to perfect it. Saw a guy do the same thing in the Bronx one time with a tin can, rubber, and some steel wool."

"So maybe he's not a genius." Mac raised his eyebrows, and nodded as if to ask, "That's good right?"

"Woo-hoo, go our team," Hunts said, sarcastically. He stuck his finger in his mouth and made a popping sound. "Sorry I didn't steal a champagne cart, guys."

Coco stood up. She looked from Hunts to Crankshaft. Her posture stiffened as she put her glass down on the beer cart and walked to face Mac. Her eyes glowing with revelation, she smiled and looked right into Mac's.

"He *is* doing it with sound."

Mac's head tilted like the RCA Victor dog.

"Don't you see?" Coco pointed from one to the other of them. "Resonance! He's using resonance! The part of my act where I break a wine glass with my voice, I have to find the resonant tone of the crystal to shatter it. Sometimes I have to waver the note to hit just the right tone. You ever play the piano at somebody's house, and every time you hit a certain note the room shakes? That's because that one particular note is the resonant tone of the room."

"So you think this guy has found some way to aim sound at somebody till they just vibrate to death?"

"With a name like Resonance, I'd say it's likely." Coco looked from one to the other. They nodded in agreement.

Mac looked at his watch for the hundredth time, then gave Hunts a look that could only be described as imperative. "You're the reporter. What have we got?"

"Well…who, what, where, when, how." Hunts said, reviewing the journalist's guide to fact. He pulled the pencil out of the edge of his mouth and began reading from a pad full of doodles.

"Who? Some guy named Resonance who might, or might not be, the guy with the goatee, some gangster types, and the fairgoers. What? Killing for ransom. 'Where' is here, the World's Fair. 'When' is now. And, 'How' is with intimidation and murder. Some sort of sound gun or device, guns with baffling silencers, mufflers, whatever the expert here wants to call them." He waved his pencil at Crankshaft.

"But why?" Coco said.

"Money," Crankshaft answered, "Power, vengeance maybe...or insanity. In a world that makes sense you don't just start killing people you never met."

"Vengeance," Mac said, his voice quiet but chilling. "He wants the money, but he's killing people out of resentment... And if you're mad at the world, what better place than the World's Fair." Mac looked at his watch again. "We've got maybe thirty-minutes."

"*If* he follows his own instructions," Hunts said, "and that's a big if, he's gonna whack somebody in the State or Federal Buildings on the north side."

"Cops have the place sewn up," Crankshaft answered. "There's a small army of uniforms and undercover out there."

"To Serve And Collect," Mac deadpanned. "For all we know, one of the cops could be in on it. If I had time, I'd like to go over there, but I think we need to find a way to get the crowd out of here."

"He said, he'd kill 'em all," Hunts reminded him.

"So I don't think it's a very good idea letting 'em hang around." Mac leaned back against the far wall, where the policemen on duty below couldn't see him, and, more out of habit than out of need, flipped open the drum of his revolver to check the ammo.

"How are you going to evacuate them?" Crankshaft walked back to join Coco and everybody formed a circle.

"I don't know," Mac said, flipping the chamber closed and sticking the gun back in his shoulder holster. "Maybe we should just blow something up and scare 'em all off."

"So they run for the exits," Crankshaft almost laughed. "And Mister Sound Wave blasts them all at once."

Mac sighed. "You got a point, but that's what's bugging me. If this guy's secret weapon can burn through a person, couldn't he just unleash it on some of the exhibits by changing the notes? Guy could collapse the Sky Ride and have anything he wants, instantly. He's playing with us."

"What are you going to do?"

Mac noticed Crankshaft hadn't included himself in the plan yet.

"Play with him. There's not a whole lot we can do over at the State build-ings, anyway, except get arrested. This may be our only chance. Let's go see who's guarding the 23rd Street gate. Maybe we can blow them up. "

A series of nods and shrugs spoke for the rest of them.

Mac lit a cigarette, stared out the window into the darkness, then turned and walked on down the hall.

✳ ✳ ✳

Hunts Helms and Coco had decided to perform reconnaissance, reporting whatever might happen at the State and Federal buildings. Mac and Crankshaft stood just inside the exit gates, watching a few late night ticket holders arrive and others depart in small groups.

"I'm guessing orders are to shoot if the crowd begins to stampede." Mac said, sipping from a paper cup.

"If he's not just bluffing," Crankshaft reasoned. "Or he could have some kind of sniper nearby. Maybe even across the street."

"Let's hope not." Mac eyed the buildings on the other side of Michigan Avenue and the several men and children loitering outside the gate. He tossed his empty paper cup into a trash can, and stepped toward the edge of the Fair's shimmering lights.

Crankshaft watched as Mac idled up to several boys tossing a baseball around and talking trash by a park bench just off the entrance.

"You guys want to make enough money to spend all day at the park tomorrow?" Mac said, and got the attention of a boy in baggy slacks. When the oldest boy in long pants turned, so did the line of them. Mac waved his arm and soon, three kids stood in front of him with their hands on their hips, listening. Mac said something, handed them some money in bills, big money for a kid, and then walked back toward the entrance. The boys went back into a huddle, and Mac ran through the entrance gate waving his ticket stub. With no line, the whole thing had taken less than five minutes.

"Now wait, and watch," Mac said, tilting his hat at a jaunty angle, and leaning over the four-foot rail by the gate like he was waiting for a sporting event to begin.

Crankshaft knew better than to ask.

A boy in long pants and a baseball cap stood up from the street urchins huddle. Mac gave him the thumbs up and pointed at two men in two-hundred dollar suits across the path, leaning against the fence. The boy said something to the others, and the huddle broke up as the rest of the boys watched in a line, leaning and pushing against each other like a pack of feral animals, which is kind of what they were.

The boy in long pants looked to be about ten years old and already out-growing last years clothes. He set the brim of his cap down low on his head, stepped across the path and stood directly in front of one of the well-tailored men, who was waving a toothpick like a crowbar in front of his teeth.

The boy kicked him in the shin and yelled. "I know all about your resonant sound machine, mister! I ain't scared of ya!"

The man in the Panama dropped his toothpick, wrapped his hands around his shin, and began hopping up and down. The boy ran away from the fair entrance and stopped at the corner to yell "Chicken!" then disappeared around a bank of hedges.

The man in the Panama hat limped after him a few paces and gave up. He tried to walk off the pain, but had to stop and clutch his leg again, his friend pointing and laughing at him all the while.

"I don't think those are our guys," Mac said, idling over to a knothole in the clapboard fence.

"That OK, boss?" the kid said from the bushes on the other side of the fence.

"Perfect." Mac shoved a dollar bill through the knothole, waved to a second boy, and stepped back out on the pathway.

Crankshaft eyed him sidewise. "You enjoy corrupting people, don't you?"

"One man's corruption is a kid's even break," Mac said. "Look at what they're wearing, Crank. They're on their own. Leastways now they'll be able to eat."

"They?"

"Show's not over." Mac leaned forward to get a glimpse through the clump of bushes.

As if on cue, a boy in knickers and a flat cap stepped on the pathway, stopped and set his cap just like the older boy before him had. About twenty feet beyond the two men in suits, on a bench across the outside path, sat a man in a sport shirt and straw fedora. He carried a pen and a small notebook he constantly jotted notes in, but he looked more like a bookie than a writer.

The second boy, all of eight years old, leaned forward and broke into a mad dash straight at the bookie. He kicked him in the shin, stood there looking directly into the man's eyes and hollered.

"I know all 'bout your res'nant sound machine, mister! I ain't a'scared of ya!"

The bookie grabbed him by the wrist with a quick hand, but the kid twisted out of his grip and slid across the path on his belly. The pencil and notebook spun in the air and slid on the concrete. The bookie's hand shot back out and grappled the boy by the ankle. The boy flipped on one side, and an arm reached, grappling for something. He came up holding the pencil like a dagger and stuck it in back of the man's hand.

The bookie screamed, staring at his hand for a moment, his eyes wide with shock. Gingerly grabbing the pencil, he yanked it out, cursing between clenched teeth. The boy reached the bushes on the corner and jeered.

"Chickie! Chickie! Cocka-doodle-doo!" He stuck both thumbs in his ears and waved his hands.

The bookie didn't even bother with him, just stood there holding his wounded hand.

"Probably not one of our guys either," Mac said, then looked at Crankshaft. "I really didn't think the kids would hurt any of these guys."

"Tough kids," Crankshaft said.

"Tough city. I think that must've been the middle child of the family try-ing to stand out."

"What's your excuse?" Crankshaft stuck both hands in his pockets.

Mac opened his mouth and stuck a finger in the air as if to respond, but never said anything. The middle child whistled lightly from the other side of the fence.

"That OK?"

"'S'alright," Mac said, shoving another bill through the knothole in the fence. "Try not to hurt 'em next time."

"He almost caught me," the boy said, as the bill disappeared.

Mac looked up at Crankshaft. Crankshaft stared at Mac. Both of them trying to understand the other and failing miserably.

"One more," Mac said.

Crankshaft realized if he kept rolling his eyes he was going to get a headache.

The next boy stepped out, and this time the ace mechanic and the illicit detective glanced at each other in complete understanding. *What the hell was Mac thinking?*

The kid couldn't have been more than six years old. He stood about three feet tall, wore a baggy red sweater four sizes too big and no hat. He pushed stringy blonde bangs out of his face and they immediately fell back down in his eyes.

Across the path, about ten feet from where the two men in expensive suits had been, stood a barely noticeable man in a khaki uniform. Standing behind a maintenance cart, he might have been with the fairground's crew but most of them wore gray and at least bothered to push a broom; this guy was wearing a mechanic's jacket in July. He'd simply push the maintenance cart a few feet, and then push it back, stopping every once in a while to reach underneath and pull out his hand with a bag wrapped around it.

The tiny first-grader-turned-wiseguy gritted his teeth, and slung the hair out his eyes again. Then ran right up next to the man in khaki, and kicked him in the shin, hard. At first the man in khaki reacted like he had a prosthetic leg, looking down to see what might have shaken him. The edges of his mouth twisted up in a crooked smile as if he could identify with the little boy. Then the boy screamed.

"I know all 'bout your residence sound machine, mister, and I ain't a'scared!"

That got the iron-shinned man's attention. His right hand made a reach for the little wiseguy.

The boy ducked it and twirled, snarling, "Pansy," as the khaki man's arms grappled empty air.

Mac slapped himself in the side of the jaw. The kid was only supposed to say he wasn't scared, not serve himself up for slaughter. Then, something funny happened.

The man made a second reach, but the boy slid away, cackling all the while like some kind of demented midget as he ducked into the hedges, before even trying to make for the far corner. Instead of giving chase or hopping or crying for help, the khaki man reached under his cart again. His hand never reappeared, but popped back out covered by a small paper bag. The man held the bag in front of his face, and began speaking to it.

He was holding some sort of two-way radio, a walkie-talkie. Mac had already noticed the police at the fair only had radios at specific stations and, for the most part, used police call boxes. And who was going to give an expensive piece of equipment like a walkie-talkie to a janitor, anyway?

"That could be our man," Mac muttered, over his shoulder at Crankshaft and edged up to the fence. He stuck another dollar bill in the knothole. This time it disappeared without a word. He looked between the shrubs and over the fence. The man in khaki was facing the other direction, still talking to the bag covering his hand. Then he signaled, waving the other hand in the air, turned around quickly and looked directly at Mac.

Mac still had a thief's instinct for dodging eye-contact. He ducked and backed toward the path, where he turned, pulled a cigarette out of a beaten pack and stuck it in the corner of his mouth. Again, he opened his mouth to say something to Crankshaft, but when he looked up all he could see were gun barrels pointed at him.

They were surrounded by security guards. A Thompson, a handful of automatics, a shotgun, even a switchblade knife.

"Crank, remember what I said about the cops?" Gun hammers cocked and ratcheted around them as the two men raised their hands. "I'm thinking maybe Security could be in on it."

Crankshaft mouthed a string of obscenities.

"I'm thinking maybe security could be in on it."

Chapter Eight
WOLVES AT THE GATE

"Whoa, guys," Mac said, almost shrugging, his hands still at shoulder level. "We were just standing here on the pathway, waiting for our friends." He waved a hand toward the space behind them. The Security Guards flinched and then smiled collectively. Mac may have stood six-feet tall, but he wasn't all that intimidating unless he was angry. No, these night watchmen were looking for somebody tough.

And Mac with that con-man's corn-fed look of befuddlement, that near stuttering "Aw shucks, guys" grin on his face; there was no way he could possibly be that man. Five of the six men turned toward the wiry black man still asking questions and mouthing obscenities to everybody within hearing distance. That was the guy that looked like trouble.

The guard behind Mac held a Thompson sub-machine gun. Modified for war, it was also perfect for Chicago. McCullough could feel its barrel pressing into the middle of his back a little harder, as the guard leaned forward trying to look over Mac's shoulder and see the show Crankshaft was putting on.

One of the guards put a .45 automatic in Crankshaft's face, and the ace mechanic slapped the barrel away. Across the path, Mac felt the gun dig in his back a little harder. The guard was watching the show.

The Man of Steal pitched himself forward, landing on his hands. His legs slid backward, wrapping around his captor's. The guard hardly had time to notice until Mac flipped sideways and grabbed the Tommy gun barrel. The security guard's hip struck the pavement, and the ex-mobster twisted the chopper out of his hands. Mac rammed the Thompson's butt off the man's head, and in one fluid movement rolled into the bushes with his finger in the trigger guard and the stock on his shoulder.

Crankshaft had turned from the guard whose gun he'd slapped away only seconds ago, holding his hands out as if to say he wasn't looking for a fight. When the man in blue turned to see the commotion Mac was causing, Crankshaft leapt sideways and kicked him in the head. The ace mechanic had the man's gun in his hand before his opponent hit the concrete.

But when he looked up, Crankshaft was surrounded. One man was face down on the concrete, but Mac was nowhere to be seen. Four to one. Crankshaft raised his hands but held onto the automatic. One of the men motioned with a shotgun for him to drop it. The fingers on Crankshaft's right hand opened, and another man stepped forward, gingerly trying to take the gun from him.

Crankshaft waved an arm, grabbed the man's hand by the base of the thumb and twisted, forcing the guard to his knees. He shoved the gun into the side of guard's head, only to look up into the barrels of three more. Two automatics and a shotgun. The man with the shotgun's finger tightened on the trigger.

From out of nowhere, a burst of machine-gun fire kicked up the concrete at the feet of the guard brandishing the shotgun. The guard turned to aim and saw only madness.

At first it looked like the Tommy-gunner didn't have a face, then the guard realized it was a mask. Cold comfort at best, because the steel blue eyes behind the mask were all the more frightening if one considered that an actual human might be in charge of them. A ribbon of smoke trailed from the Thompson's barrel, wrapping around the masked man's head like Satan's scarf. And smoldering beneath the band of smoke, two eyes burned, like blue gas fires buried in the shadows beneath the bill of a fedora.

Then he laughed, if you could call it that. It was the laughter of the damned, and it bordered somewhere between angry and hysteric, between a scream and a growl, pain and revenge.

In his peripheral vision, the shaken security guard saw one of his partners sink to the ground, shot by Crankshaft the instant the machine gun had gone off. The black man popped the butt of his .45 off the head of the guard he already held captive by the thumb, and came up with his automatic aimed at the head of the guard watching him. The two men stood at point blank range, arms extended, frozen.

Two to two.

"Security my ass," The Bagman said, from behind the Thompson's barrel. His voice was cold and low. He stepped forward with the Tommy-gun pointed at the face of the guard wielding the shotgun, turned to look at Crankshaft, and smiled under the mask. It was the kind of smile a cat gets while it's playing with a mouse's corpse.

"You hit me right between the eyes with that thing," he said to the man aiming the shotgun, "I'm still not going to die instantly. All those little pellets hit me at this range, I'm gonna spasm. And when I do, I'm going to cut you in half."

The guard with the shotgun glanced over at the guard with the .45 auto, who was much too occupied by Crankshaft to notice.

The voice behind the mask said, "Now comes the easy part. You drop your guns and walk away or you die."

The crowd around the 23rd Street Plaza had all but disappeared, which is what Mac had wanted to begin with. Other than a few people hidden behind a souvenir stand, most of the crowd was gathered outside the entrance. The Bagman wandered leisurely in a circle, the Thompson gun still aimed at the guard wielding the shotgun. The masked man's back was never to the crowd for more than a moment.

The calliope sounds of the Midway and its hucksters stood out against the silence of the four men in a Mexican standoff, all with guns primed to kill at the slightest jump. The man with the .45 switched off, aiming at The Bagman for a moment, then back at Crankshaft again. Sweat trailed down the side of his face.

The Bagman strode defiantly at the man with the shotgun. "You gonna pull that trigger, or you just going to stand there and shake." He put the Thompson's gun stock to his shoulder, and aimed at the man's chest. "I'll go first…"

For a moment the carnival sounds of the Midway and the crowd all around seemed to blur into the background. Then, Mac heard the distinctive ratcheting sound of a gun being cocked, and something pressed against the back of his head.

They'd completely forgotten about the man in khaki who'd been on the two way radio; the man now standing behind Mac, and pressing a .38 Colt Special against the base of his skull.

The Bagman glanced at Crankshaft, who was pressing the air with one of his hands, telling Mac not to move. Mac was about to turn around anyway and say something to the man in khaki, maybe ask him about his walkie-talkie, anything to keep him confused, when something behind him went thud.

He heard the body slap the pavement and glanced at Crankshaft again. The ace mechanic was still patting the air, but his mouth was wide open and looking at whatever was behind The Bagman.

"Nobody moves," a voice behind Mac said.

The Bagman turned around anyway and found himself staring down the barrel of a big, mean .45 automatic.

Behind the .45 was a big, mean man in a black mask.

"Drop the chopper," said the man. He pressed the barrel of his .45 against The Bagman's forehead.

The Bagman lowered his Thompson to the side, gripping its barrel like a soldier on drill. He shifted his head around the man in black's .45, trying to get a look into his eyes.

The man was taller than Mac. He wore a wide-brimmed fedora. The hat band matched the mask that hung over half the stranger's face, and underneath his heavy over coat was a three-piece suit and twin shoulder holsters. Another pearl-handled automatic sat holstered there with the leather hammer strap still snapped over it. The man in black hadn't even bothered to pull both guns.

"Don't bother to shoot, Crank. It wouldn't do any good anyway," The Bagman said. He held one finger up, still swiveling his head around, trying to make eye contact with the gunman, looking more like a man playing with a kaleidoscope than a man with a gun barrel between his eyes.

The man in the black mask kept rotating the barrel around Mac's head, but otherwise remained still.

"Excuse me," The Bagman said, and slung the machine gun over his head like an axe thrower executing a hook shot. The Thompson whirled through the air and bounced off the head of the security guard holding the shotgun. The guard went down, dropping the gun. He was stunned but not out.

"That guy!" Mac pointed with his throwing arm "...was just going to be trouble!"

The wobbly guard flopped around on the concrete some more, and came up reaching for the scattergun.

"Don't," warned the man in the black mask, his gun now aimed at the unsteady guard on the pavement.

Taking advantage of the distraction, Crankshaft snatched the automatic out of the remaining guard's hand. The guard simply stood there, looking down the barrel of the ace mechanic's gun. Crankshaft took two more steps and kicked the shotgun toward The Bagman. The Bagman just stood there, not even reaching for it. Instead he waved an arm of introduction toward the other masked man.

"Crank, meet The Black Wolf," he said, "who hopefully realizes real security guards rarely carry shotguns."

✳ ✳ ✳

The Black Wolf, Avenger of Granton City, whose two-fisted, cross-draw wielded the ultimate justice in a city that had once been the major artery of the North American black market. Throughout the twenties The Black Wolf had rolled over bootleggers and gun smugglers like a juggernaut, assigning himself as judge, jury, and sometimes executioner in a city that law had abandoned.

"Another guy with a mask on," Crankshaft said. "Great, there are two of you. I'll look twice as stupid when I end up in jail."

"I don't think The Wolf is gonna want us in jail," The Bagman said, "What brings you to the city of big shoulders, Wolfie?"

The Black Wolf frowned, his eyebrows visibly forming a "V" beneath the mask. He tilted his head, just the slightest to the side.

"McCullough," he muttered in realization. "Mac Mc—"

"Sshhhhhhht!" The Bagman started to clamp one hand over The Black Wolf's mouth, but having seen the look on his face, decided it might be better to signal with a finger in front of his own lips. Mac walked toward the guard who'd been holding the shotgun, and hit him on the head with the butt of his revolver.

Crankshaft spun his man around and clubbed him behind the ear.

Both The Black Wolf and The Bagman began to notice the surroundings, people were gathering around again. Mac held his six-shooter up in the air and pulled the trigger till it was empty. The gawkers thinned, to put it mildly.

"Don't panic the crowd," The Black Wolf said.

"Don't panic me." Crankshaft said, strolling by the two men and tucking a .45 into his belt.

"Just making some space," Mac said, thumbing more bullets into his revolver.

The two masked men backed away from the pathway, their faces disappearing behind the hedge at the exact same moment a platoon of policeman burst out of the Heidelberg Inn, trying to get a better view of the plaza where all the shooting came from. Leaning against the back of one of the ticket booths, Mac pulled off his mask, and looked at his watch.

Fifteen minutes to another murder.

"C'mon, Wolf. If we want to catch these guys; we need to get over to the State Building."

"You're crazy, McCullough." The Black Wolf pointed his gun at Mac's head.

"You *do* know him!" Crankshaft said in mock surprise, his .45 already pressed against The Wolf's temple.

"And you're getting to know Crank," Mac said, staring into The Black Wolf's eyes and grinning. "That's so cute. Really, it is. Crank spent half the war on the Western Front, y'know. He's really good at killing people."

"We on the square?" Crankshaft stepped in front of The Black Wolf and holstered his gun.

The Black Wolf could have drawn both his twin pearl handled automatics but didn't. Instead, he sighed and holstered his gun.

"What's the deal with that 'on the square stuff?" Mac said. "Why is it if a deal's on the up-and-up it's 'on the square,' but when it goes bad it's a 'square deal?'"

Crankshaft and The Black Wolf looked at him like he was from outer space.

"Never mind," Mac said, blankly "We've gotta move."

"How am I supposed to believe anything that comes out of your mouth,

McCullough? Last time I saw you, you were bilking people out of fortunes, posing as some sort of Sikh medicine man, Artough Singh..."

"Hey, Mr. Singh made good money giving greedy bastards advice." Mac stood up and straightened his jacket like he'd just been accused of spiking the punch at a party. "It's not my fault they figured out Artough wasn't an Indian name! Look, Wolf, I know you don't have any reason to believe me, but I'm trying to do the right thing. I'm playing for the good guys."

"The Bagman." The Wolf's voice was ice. "You blew up a street with a hand grenade and took hostages..."

"Those hostages were part of a protection racket," Mac was talking fast now.

"In case you hadn't noticed, 'the kid' also took out an entire branch of Nitti's mob, and a gang of crooked cops," Crankshaft added. "The news hawks aren't exactly front-paging those narratives."

"OK, McCullough. Granted you were always weird and, you were the only con man I ever saw steal from people worse than he was but why should I trust a man who can't be trusted?"

"Because some bad men tried to take out one of my own." Mac looked at his watch again. "And because justice isn't always about the law, Wolf."

As Crankshaft and the Black Wolf exchanged glances, a slight thrum echoed in the distance, barely noticeable except for a low bass tone. Dogs from south and west of the city across Michigan Avenue began barking. Ignoring Crank and The Wolf, Mac stepped back on the pathway and stretched his neck in two directions. Pugs in royal wardrobe from the China exhibit barked at the sky, while the goats in India brayed. A low background of bleats, bays, and roars seemed to rise from every exhibit in the world.

The Black Wolf pulled up the collar of his chain-mail trench coat, obscuring his face, and stepped out on the path to join The Bagman. Crankshaft looked at his watch, pacing back and forth between the two men toward the Federal and State Buildings.

A black cloud, darker than the night, hung in the sky.

The Black Wolf pointed out over the lake. "An airship... no, a blimp."

"Hindenburg won't be here for months," Mac said. "Hey, Crank, what time's the Good Year Blimp supposed to fly over."

"Three in the afternoon."

"Late, without lights, and aimed right the Federal Building," Mac said. "Looks like 'the sky's the limit' means death from above."

Chapter Nine
RACE AGAINST CRIME

The fairgrounds visibly darkened as a low bass sound echoed over the lake, making the myriad lights on the fairground seem brighter. The blimp was visible only because of the tiny piece of sky it blanked out as it grew larger, coming closer.

"We've got to stop that thing," The Bagman said.

"How?" Crankshaft looked at his watch. "We've got maybe ten minutes."

"Why?" said the Black Wolf.

Mac looked around. The tallest thing on the fairground besides The Sky Ride was the arrow-shaped Havoline Thermometer, the world's largest, standing some two-hundred-and-eighteen feet high.

"Hey! We could always blow some dynamite under the giant thermometer; maybe shoot that thing out of the sky!" Mac said, smiling. Crankshaft couldn't tell whether he was serious or not.

"It's not aerodynamic and it weighs a ton. You know how much mercury is in that thing? Plus you'd need some way to aim…"

"I was just kiddin', Crank."

"What are you people even talking about?" The Wolf said, still eyeing the shadow of the airship above the lake as the insidious drone of its engine mixed with the Midway's calliopes and ringing bells.

"There's an airport hangar just south of the hangar where they keep the blimp." Mac waved his arm. "You know how to fly a plane Wolf?"

"Sure, but…"

"I'll explain on the way," Mac said.

The Wolf pulled his collar up and began to head south. Mac grabbed him by the arm.

"Whoa, slow down there, cowboy," he said, steering The Wolf in the other direction. "You just gonna stroll right by the Old Heidelberg where all the cops are waiting? That collar could cover your head, and you'd still stand out in the crowd."

"I don't have a problem with the police. We need a car," The Wolf said.

"We don't have time to go out in the lot and steal one," Crankshaft said. "Much less, time to explain things to the cops and you," he added with a scowl.

Mac scanned the plaza just inside the gate by the 23rd Street entrance. Some rickshaws stood parked across the street. Service trucks hauling hay for animals. A horse was tied outside Egypt. Mac didn't feel like riding two men on a horse, and he sure as hell knew the Wolf wasn't going to pull him around in a rickshaw.

Fortunately, General Motors had commissioned more than two-hundred open sided buses for the fair, and one of them sat on the other side of the plaza. Eight passengers were already seated, waiting for the bus driver to start his shift or come back from a break.

"I've got an idea," Mac said.

"I'm heading over to the Federal Building and warn the crowd," Crankshaft said. He didn't like a lot of Mac's ideas.

"OK, Wolf. Just give me the benefit of the doubt until I can explain."

The Black Wolf gave him a look of nothing but doubt.

"C'mon, we're taking the bus." Mac grabbed The Wolf by the arm again, while The Granton City Avenger was still in the middle of a double-take.

The Wolf shook Mac's hand off and followed, more out of curiosity than commitment. Mac sprung up the tour bus's steps, where he stood with arms outstretched as if to welcome the riders and allow The Wolf to pass. The Wolf sat down behind the driver's seat, ready to exit at any instance. Mac grabbed the radio microphone and, while waving his hand to the riders already seated, sat down behind the wheel.

"Ladies and gentleman!" he said, and smiled when the echoing voice broadcast from the P.A. caught up with his own. "Welcome to Chicago's Columbian Exposition and World's Fair. This bus will be running express to The World of Transportation and beyond!"

Mac revved the engine before his voice stopped, then honked the horn, and peeled out across the plaza. Crossing from a parking space on the left and into the right lanes, he cut off a bus ahead of him. The other bus hit the brakes and fishtailed to the left barely missing the back of Mac's. Packs of fairgoers ran, screaming and pushing to get out of the way. Mac kept honking the horn, and the bus flew down Leif Erickson Drive. He ran a stop sign, almost hit a brand new Nash, and a couple of families, then grabbed the mike again.

"Ladies and Gentlemen, on your left was India! Coming up…The Midway!"

Passengers were too busy hanging on to stop and look. Mac hung the mouthpiece back on its prongs, and explained the situation as quickly as he could to The Wolf.

"We've got a terrorist thing here. Only this guy makes the I.R.A. look like amateurs. He's using some kind of sound cannon."

The Wolf narrowed one eye, and leaned forward. "Fascists?"

"Could be, but our local krauts aren't too sympathetic to their homeland's turn of heart. Lindbergh may like 'em but personally, I don't like the whole Charlie Chaplin mustache thing. I always thought Buster Keaton was funnier."

The Wolf nodded, almost smiled. "You know, I wouldn't believe you for a second if you'd opened up on those goons with that Tommy-gun? Instead, you shoot at the ground, scare the bejeezus out of everybody screaming like a crazy man, and nobody innocent got hurt. Pretty good."

Mac slammed on the brakes as a band of tourists pitched themselves into a ditch to avoid getting hit. The whole bus went up on its front wheels. Everybody slid out of their seats.

"But I still don't trust you," The Black Wolf said, pushing himself back up.

Mac smiled and grabbed the mike.

"On your left are balloon rides, on the right is a shooting gallery, Fort Dearborn, The Vienna Café, an Indian Village." He was talking so fast it all became one long word. "Home and Industrial Arts Anthropology The Mayan Temple and GeneralMotors! A Pageant of Transportation!"

The Wolf's eyes narrowed. One minute he was talking to a rational man and the next a vaudeville act. Mac hung the mike back up, put both hands on the wheel and floored it. A rickshaw driver skittered across the path, barely making it out of the way and spilling his passenger on the other side of the road.

Mac was glad he'd taken the bus.

"Think what you want, Wolf. I don't care. As far as firepower, I don't like using what I carry. But thanks to this Resonance character I had to kill some people today; they were lousy people, but…" He downshifted and bus gears grinded. "Bottom line is, if that blimp reaches the Federal or States Buildings before we do, more people are gonna die. I'd rather just kill the guy trying to kill them."

"I'd be more willing to trust you, if there weren't warrants all over Chicago regarding The Bagman and the rackets," The Black Wolf said.

"Wolf, this is Chicago. You hear about anybody willing to step forward and press charges?"

"People are afraid to testify against the rackets."

"Especially when there isn't one. Look, Wolf, if I run the mob out of town and don't pretend to steal their thunder, how long do you think it's going to be till the next mob takes over…? Don't forget folks, the Travel and Transport Building means trains, ships, automobiles and planes!"

Mac had picked up the mike and started announcing even as the realization of his words lighted up in The Wolf's eyes.

"McCullough, don't expect me to make things easy for you, but this terrorist; he might be tied in with my fascists. The President has National Security all over the Hindenburg Landing here this fall, but what if the German Bund wanted to demonstrate their power another way? Trashing the World's Fair with futuristic science could frighten a lot of people into submission."

"Yeah, or it could just be another racket," Mac said, still holding the microphone. "On your left...Look out!"

Mac hopped the bus's right wheels over the curb, dodging a baby carriage. The bus swerved back on the road, tearing down a long string of lighting that popped and sparked, cascading behind them till the long, fraying wires dragged nothing but the shards of empty glass in the sockets. The people in back screamed as the cords whipped at the open sides of the bus.

"And don't forget to visit the National Poultry Council!" Mac said, as he veered the bus in the other direction, straight down the dead end where the Goodyear Hangar stood. "Please remain seated for your safety."

At sixty-miles-an-hour the tour bus hit the curb at a right angle, popping the front tires and grinding to a stop on the lawn sixty feet later.

Mac had both hands clamped on the wheel. He turned slowly to look at the riders. Five were left. Three were still conscious, but looked a little sea sick. He hoped the three people he'd lost had jumped and not fallen out.

The Black Wolf leaped out of the bus ahead of him. Mac, strangely enough, remained seated, his eyes wandering back and forth across the dashboard. As The Wolf stood outside watching, Mac pulled a small bicycle tool out of his pocket. He aimed the screwdriver at the corners of the microphone's hardware, and pried it out of the dashboard. When he was finished, The Bagman had wrenched a condenser off the radio with a wad of wires and tubes still tangled to it. There were sirens in the distance.

"C'mon," The Black Wolf said, and began to pace.

Mac stuck the condenser in his pocket, and the two men strode purposefully toward the far end of the hangar. They stuck close, with their backs to the building, staying just out of view from whoever might be inside

Peeking around the sheet metal door of the structure, they saw a gang of four men in pinstripe suits standing outside the office. But the guns in their shoulder holsters made all those pinstripes bulge, and at second glance it was evident they weren't just standing; they were standing guard. Two airplanes stood parked close to the door of the hangar. Another man in coveralls was cleaning off the tool bench. The Black Wolf reached for his shoulder holsters.

"If we can flank them from behind on both sides..."

"There'll be a lot of shooting, and people will get killed by guns that go 'sput.' Let me handle this Wolf. I've got an I.D. card."

"I.D.?" The Black Wolf kept his hands on his guns.

"This is the part where I use what I learned being a bad man...on bad men."

The Wolf dropped one hand and nodded.

Mac left his mask off. His goal was to look like one of the gang. He ran in place a moment, nodded at The Black Wolf, and then came running out in front of the open hangar door like a projectile. He waved a hand from outside to get their attention, then stopped and leaned over with his hands on his knees as if he was trying to catch his breath.

Two of the men drew automatics. Mac didn't flinch. Instead he stumbled toward them.

"We got trouble!" He reached out and touched the arm of one of the gunmen as if he knew him.

"YOU got trouble," one of the other goons said, slipping up behind him.

"Hold it. Hold it. Hold it!" Mac held his hands out to show he wasn't going for a gun. "I'm reaching for my…" He was reaching for the card he'd taken from the fishy photographer, the one with the word "Resonance" engraved on it next to a megaphone sprouting with tentacles.

That's when he remembered he didn't have his terrorist's membership card anymore. Because he still didn't have his wallet.

All four men had their guns aimed at him. The man in coveralls kept working at the tool bench as if this sort of thing happened all the time. Mac's pulse jumped, but he didn't let it show. Instead he leaned back, arms extended with his palms up in the universal symbol of "What are you talkin' about?"

"Guys, we don't have time for this." He reached slowly for his coat pocket. He'd planned to use the condenser if he'd had to.

He had to.

"We ain't got time to be waving our Resonance cards around and talking shop! It's an emergency!" Mac pulled out the condenser, clutching it in his fist like the world's largest diamond. "Brown was supposed to make sure they had this part onboard for the radio. Without it, there's no way to for the boss to use his tools!"

Mac hoped he was keeping it vague enough that they wouldn't catch on. Surely, there had to be somebody named Brown around.

"Brown's an idiot," a gangster sporting one eyebrow said.

"Yeah, well at this point he's gonna be a dead idiot. No transmitter, no mission. No mission, no dough. You get me?" Mac's angry voice was caused more by the men he was facing than any Mr. Brown.

Two of the gunmen remained frozen, dead eyes hanging over the sights of their guns. The other two seemed to step back without moving, their guns to the side. The men exchanged glance and shrugs.

"C'mon alreadyyyyyy!" Mac's voice was imperative. "We got it all set up, we drop the part off like the blimp is refueling in the air. What we don't have is time for you'se guys to stand around gawking." He turned around ready to call for The Black Wolf. His plan was to pass the Wolf off as if he were dressed up for some sort of circus act.

The man in coveralls straightening the tool bench turned around and looked at Mac. His eyes narrowed and looked at Mac's hand.

"They need a condenser to drop a bomb?" he said.

Mac didn't even know what a condenser was.

"All's I know is he hands me this for the radio!" Mac was screaming, holding the batch of wire and metal high in the air. "And says if we can't get it onboard, we're dead in the water! That's what he said, he said we were all gonna be dead in the water!"

"A condenser?" the man in coveralls said. He was burly and stood well above six feet. Two of the gunmen parted as he stepped forward. His burr haircut revealed a burrowed scalp as he grabbed Mac's hand to look at the radio hardware.

Mac grabbed the man by the wrist, twisted himself beneath the larger man's arm and came up behind him, forcing the man's arm behind his back. Mac's face popped up behind the man in coveralls' shoulder, his revolver pressed to the man's temple. The man in coveralls face went white.

"Look, I'm just following orders here," Mac said. "We need a plane."

The four men stood with guns aimed. One of them extended his arm a little farther and narrowed one eye, preparing to target shoot around the mechanic's head.

Mac twisted the larger man's body as the gun went off.

His hostage's head jerked and a lump of red, white and grey exploded out of the back of it. Splintered bone stung Mac's jaw. He could feel the brains on his face. He let go of the body, propping it up with his shoulder. Kneeling under the larger man's arm, The Bagman slapped leather and fanned the hammer of his six-gun like one of the bad guys in a Saturday western matinee.

Five shots. Three of the men writhed on the floor. The last one, still spinning, fell clutching at his ribcage. The Black Wolf stood just beyond the light outside the hangar, his face in the shadows except for his eyes burning behind two .45 automatics. He stepped forward and clubbed the last remaining thug on the head with the butt of his gun.

"I thought there wasn't going to be any shooting," The Wolf said.

"Damnit! Damnit! Damnit!" Mac threw his gun at the man who'd started the gunfight. "I told you guys I'd shoot him; so *you* shoot him? Smart! Real smart!"

The Black Wolf gave Mac a knowing look, but Mac wasn't talking to him.

"What's wrong with you people?" Mac was talking to himself. He looked at The Wolf and continued cursing under his breath as he crossed the room to pick up his revolver. He flipped open the chamber, emptied the casings, and shoved a handful of bullets inside. His jaw clenched, he muttered two barely audible words. The second one was "murderers."

"You OK, kid?" The Wolf asked.

Silence was his only answer.

Neither man said a word as they advanced toward a Stearman Kaydet navy flight trainer, on the side of the hangar. The double winged stunt plane was still painted yellow, but appeared to be well on its way to becoming a crop duster.

There was a moan from one of the wounded gunmen, neither The Wolf nor McCullough bothered to turn around. Mac pulled his mask out of his pocket, resembling a baseball catcher as he slung it over his face and crouched on the planes bottom wing. When The Bagman turned his head, The Black Wolf could see he was smiling now beneath the mask.

It gave him the creeps.

A moment ago, The Wolf had been wondering if Mac could make this mission, but now...now a chill hit The Wolf's spine. This McCullough kid might just be one for the psychology books.

Regardless, Mac stuck out his hand. The Wolf took it and stepped up on the wing. Climbing into the rear cockpit The Wolf could feel the eerie quiet of the hangar.

"I've never seen anybody fan a six-gun like that outside of Hoot Gibson. You learn that on your own?" he said.

"First time I ever tried it," The Bagman said. He stepped down off the wing and walked toward the gloom behind the tail of the plane, then stepped back out of the shadows with a monkey wrench in one hand and a small pick-axe in the other. "I figured with four of 'em, I better shoot quick and hope. This is one of those learn while you earn programs. Speaking of which," he dumped the tools in the rear cockpit, and pointed with his head toward the propeller, "I gotta go spin that thing?"

"Auto-ignition," The Wolf said.

Mac was already halfway in his seat. "C'mon. Let's go. We're outta' time."

"How you going to stop them," The Wolf said, turning in his seat.

"Don't worry," Mac said. "I have a plan."

Chapter Ten
A FLYING LEAP

The Black Wolf hit the ignition and steered the plane out of the hangar like it was on rails. A short runway sat across the field where they moored the Goodyear Blimp for takeoff. A steady wind from the South forced him to spin the plane around before hitting the runway. The Wolf hard-lined it down the tiny airstrip, wheels bouncing, once, twice, before hitting the end of the runway and bounding into the air.

The Wolf steered the stunt-plane into a tail wind, aiming it due North, directly at the dark, shadowy outline of the unlit airship. The Bagman sat buckled in his seat with goggles and no helmet, just the mask blowing in the wind. Mac smiled and shivered. He had never been in a plane before.

The only thing more amazing than the lights and flurry of The World's Fair was seeing it from the air and then seeing it from above Lake Michigan. From the lake the Hall of Science was a piece artwork, the merging of art deco architecture withy every color in the spectrum lined up like the notes on a kid's day-glow xylophone. The ships in the lagoons looked like Christmas ornaments and The Sky Ride's wires were the tinsel.

While the city just across Michigan Avenue seemed a murky pool lit in neon dashes, the World's Fair Exposition was an explosion of color garnered in pinpoints of white light. Entire facades shined in projected colors, while stark razors of yellow high beams in the center rotated in the skies, sending notice to life on other planets that Chicago was the center of the world. Yet the beams never struck the phantom airship over the lake.

Mac had trouble spotting the State and Federal Buildings on the North side of the fairgrounds, which was strange because both buildings were housed in a triangular complex representing the three branches of government. The lighting and bright colors normally made the buildings stand out. Straining his eyes, he spotted the government buildings; a dark spot on the fairgrounds. Crowds milled around in the plaza across the path. Somebody, probably Crankshaft, had alerted the authorities. They were evacuating the building; but most of the crowd had considered it too early to head home for the night.

When Mac looked up, the ominous silhouette of the phantom airship stood starkly in front of the plane. The apparition's shadow fell across the faces of the flying masked men, twisting their expressions with black-and-white severity. Even from behind, The Bagman could see The Wolf's jaw

...seeing it from the air...

muscles tighten. Mac held on and the plane swooped low.

The Bagman saw the muzzle flash of sparks by the dirigible's gondola. A bullet whizzed by his ear. The airplane spun hard to the right, in a twirling dive. For a second Mac thought they were going to crash.

Now it was The Black Wolf's turn to laugh. The Granton City Avenger sent the stunt-plane into a spinning dive, before pulling up, and then buzzing across the top of the lake. Alerted by the distinct sound of the Kaydet's propellor, the crowds near the shoreline took notice of the swerving stunt plane. A few hands pointed from the undulating crowd below, suddenly aware of the black hole in the sky and the thrum of the airship's engine.

The Black Wolf, wielding the stick like an expert, aimed the biplane straight up in a perpendicular line. Bullets flashed from a machinegun muzzle in the control car of the blimp. The Bagman let go with a rebel yell as they sped by, looping around the airship. Muzzle flashes tripled as bullets swarmed round the plane like hornets.

Having steered within a hundred yards of the ship they were much too close for safety, but having seen the arsenal erupting onboard, The Black Wolf could only try to avoid the next surprise. Then, with the airship's gas-bag blocking the view from its gondola, The Wolf did something amazing.

He hung the plane in the air. The mobile little Kaydet just sat in one place, hanging straight beneath its propeller like a helicopter, with the blimp's balloon between it and the machineguns. While the sound of the Kaydet's propeller steadied, the crew of the criminal airship awaited its next swoop, never realizing it hung only a short distance away.

Crewmen circled the blimp's pilot house looking for the plane. They could hear it. It had to be there.

The Wolf patiently glided the plane away from the airship, keeping it in a vertical position and hovering east, out over the Lake. As the two pilots fell into each other's view, bullets erupted from the dirigible's control car. But the tiny Boeing stunt plane was already out of range. The Wolf leveled the craft out, and swung out even farther into a wide turn.

Mac reached behind his seat for the parachute. Then he reached under his seat. He had started pulling around the paneling next to him, before he thought about asking The Wolf. He tapped him on the shoulder from behind and screamed over the propeller.

"Where's the parachute?" Mac imitated a chute with one hand, while the other beneath it imitated a man hanging in the air.

The Wolf turned, nodded. He held the plane in a slow circle, steering the stick with his knees and began reaching around his seat. A tiny voice in the back of The Bagman's head knew what he was going to say next. Hell, not only did he know it, but he had known it from the moment he'd started searching. He thought of the words "hope against hope" the exact same moment The Black Wolf hollered:

"No chute."

Mac cursed under his breath. In a tenth of a second he'd gone from hope to a man with nothing to lose. He wiped his dirty goggles and looked at the crowds outside gathered below, standing in the lights like the bulls-eye on a target. He thought about the nightmares. His bloated Dad's corpse. All the crooked things he'd ever done to survive only to later realize he was hurting others just trying to do the same. He thought about evil, and the men that do it. The word "redemption" never entered his mind, but he weighed the life of one man, not necessarily a good one, against that of hundreds, maybe thousands. He was tired, angry, depressed, lonely, and just plain mean.

It crossed his mind that he didn't add up to much, but since he'd put on the mask he'd learned his only one honest talent:

Sometimes it takes something bad to take out something even worse.

Comforting himself with that thought, he picked up the wrench in one hand and the pick axe with the other. He dropped the monkey wrench back on the floor, took a few one handed hammer swings with the pick-axe, and then massaged his grip on the handle.

"Think you can do this?" The Wolf still had no idea what Mac's plan was.

Mac barely heard him. "YOU dive in and that bullet proof coat of yours will sink like a lead weight!" he yelled.

The Wolf simply shook his head. Mac stared down over the edge of the cockpit. He tapped The Wolf on the shoulder again. The Wolf craned his head.

The Windy City Masked Man made a fist representing the airship, then held out a flat palm representing the plane. He motioned for the plane to loop over the airship, stuck a finger out and the plane became a man jumping.

The Wolf gave him a thumbs-up and the plane dropped so fast Mac felt his bladder swoop into his chest. Now he had to go to bathroom.

The Wolf flew the plane some five-hundred yards beneath the buzzing, black spot in the sky. Gunfire erupted from the airship. Neither of the masked men bothered to return fire as the speedy, little combination stunt-plane zipped beneath the starboard side of a shadow darker than the night.

The tiny Kaydet sped below, then climbed into a loop. The biplane seemed to hang in the air upside down, before twisting into a perfect Immelman turn.

Mac didn't know exactly what an Immelman Turn was, he was just glad to be right side up. Now he was sick to his stomach and he had to go to bathroom. Once again, he pushed his thoughts of personal safety aside.

You can do this, he told himself. *Give it some thought, but don't think about it.* For a second he had a mental image of himself throwing his brains out the window, followed by images of a thousand different falling deaths. He cursed as he unbuckled his safety belt, not under his breath, but loud, graphically, and into the wind. He was screaming.

And for some reason that worked for him.

Maybe because he was tired. Maybe because he hated the idea of somebody ruining a perfectly good World's Fair, or just dumping on his old hometown. Or, maybe, just maybe, he didn't care as much about himself as he did the people below. Regardless, all questioning left his mind. The flashing images of a thousand falling deaths, however, kept re-running in his head.

Fear transformed to anger. Anger transformed to righteous anger. Gather all the philosophers in the world to ponder the thoughts of one man and ultimately the only thing they would be able to agree upon was this: There was a masked man of questionable sanity climbing onto the wing of a plane, so he could jump, and try to somehow get to the control car of a killer blimp.

The first step was the worst. That being, of course, until The Bagman had to take a second step. While his left hand grasped the pickaxe, his right grappled the cross wires where they met between the wings. While his feet moved, it took every ounce of willpower he had to release his grip and gain another, so he could turn and face forward. His suit billowed around him like loose kite fabric. The wind flattened his leather mask across his face. It was hard to breathe.

Mac took one last glance down to his left before they were over the airship. Some of the people below were pointing, but nobody was running. They probably thought it was all part of some show. Straight down and to his right, Lake Michigan stood like a giant ink blot. Having never been in the air before Mac tried to do the math, and figured they were less than a mile in the air. He lied and told himself it was five-hundred feet. One last glance down convinced him he was crazy.

The Black Wolf slapped the plane's fuselage to get Mac's attention. He held up three fingers, then held up his fist, extending one finger at a time for the countdown. Mac looked down as they were almost even with the blimp. At the count of two he looked down, thinking it was already time to let go. Miscounting was no problem however, because he couldn't get his hand to open.

Mac closed his eyes, and inhaled deep. Opened them to see the Wolf hold three fingers up. He closed his eyes again. And let go.

It felt more like the plane had thrown him off, than he'd jumped. He kept both hands gripped on the pick-axe, and didn't open his eyes until it all he could feel was gravity's pull. Plummeting, he spread his arms and legs, and felt the pull lighten. From above, surrounded by the bright lights of the World's Fair, the blimp stood out like a football hanging over a gold-fish bowl.

It was coming up fast.

Mac's spread-eagled arms slowed him down, but accounting for the weight of the pick-axe had thrown him off course. He was losing trajectory. He stroked the air, kicking with his palms, swimming a half-mile in the sky. Anyone watching from below would have been startled to see a man doing the breast stroke at a thousand feet. Still flipping away from his target, Mac put his arms out in front of himself, both hands gripping the handle and shot like a bullet straight at the giant balloon.

Some three-hundred feet from the ominous dirigible, he realized there weren't any ropes running along the top of it for him to grab onto. He could try to grab one of the mooring cables over the side, but then the gunsling-ers in the blimp's cabin would just use him for target practice. He was mov-ing fast, but time moved even faster. At this rate he'd simply bounce off the balloon and drown in the lake.

He smiled beneath the mask, and realized he was laughing. This wasn't funny and he was laughing. By the time the word "hysterical" popped into his mind, The Bagman had stopped thinking. This was all reflex. He held the pick-ax out in front of him, pointing to where he wanted to go.

A hundred-and-fifty feet from the balloon, Mac could see he was aimed directly at its top center. Without the Wolf's countdown, he'd probably al-ready be in the lake. The Bagman gripped the pick-axe so hard it hurt. He spread his arms like a diver for only a moment, and then broke into a twisted pitcher's wind-up as he plummeted last ten yards.

There was nothing but gray fabric in front of him.

Falling so fast he almost didn't get his leg out of the way, Mac's right hand slung forward; breaking at the wrist like was throwing a fastball. He closed his eyes thinking if he missed he'd never open them again.

He felt the pick hit the fabric, felt its momentary resistance, then:

Pkcccrrrriiiiipt! The pick tore through part of the balloon.

The Bagman held onto the ice pick with every ounce of strength he had left and opened his eyes, just in time to see himself bouncing off the canvass and into the air. He held onto the pick even harder. Bouncing like a bull rider at a rodeo, he twisted the handle so the metal end would act as an anchor, and prayed it wouldn't lose tear loose.

Both hands on the pick handle, Mac desperately looked for something to hold onto besides the tearing fabric. No handles. No ropes. The draft from hitting the lakeshore provided more turbulence, and Mac found himself bouncing in a circular motion, his legs acting like the hands of an insane stopwatch. Gripping the hole at both sides Mac could feel the gas inside erupting out. He stuck an arm inside the balloon to get a better grip, held his breath so he wouldn't inhale any of the helium and looked inside.

Mac didn't know a lot about blimps, but reading about the fair in the paper he knew one thing. Airships, Zeppelins, those big guys, they had metal frames inside the balloon to keep it taught; blimps did not. In fact, had it not been for the invention of a flexible keel along the bottom of the blimp, they couldn't navigate. This blimp's gasbag had a thin, metal frame around the sides and top.

The masked madman stopped laughing.

A big horn like a Victrola's amplifier, stood in the middle of the gasbag, surrounded by vacuum tubes and electrical wiring. It was aimed down and forward from the ship like an express train's headlight, directly at the crowds below.

The machinery blocked his view, but around it The Bagman could see a pile of scrap metal as big as Crankshaft's entire junkyard. *Shrapnel*, Mac reasoned. Resonance's men were going to fire the cannon, and then parachute out as it collapsed. If they missed the crowd with their big sound horn, the flying scrap would still kill hundreds.

He tried to reason it out. There was no way he could reach the gondola. If he could climb inside the gasbag and find a switch, or tear up some wiring, he might be able to disarm the sound cannon. And, he'd probably just die painlessly from the gas.

He held his breath and tried anyway, but the escaping gas forced itself out at too high a pressure. He couldn't even get his head in. Meanwhile, gusts over the lake tore at his clothes, and the pick axe was already tearing a larger hole for him to squeeze through all by itself. The larger the hole got, the less he was anchored.

Mac McCullough had always been a savvy thinker, quick on his feet, thoughts racing him to the end of a big job, whether it was a long con or a six-month heist preparation. But now he was lost. He couldn't get in the balloon. Even if he could reach the cabin, he didn't have time to ask questions. A million tertiary thoughts pinballed in his head, an endless equation with no answer.

He was tired and lost. The emotions took over.

"WORLD'S FAIR! I HATE YOU!" he screamed, and almost let go of his anchor to shake a hand at the cosmos. Glancing up at the diamond stars in the darkness, he seemed to stop. A sudden sort of calm seized the man behind the mask. The frenzied movement of his eyes slowed. He looked all but dead.

"Heh." A high pitched chuckle crossed his lips. "Heh, heh," then a cackling giggle. He heard it, but never once related it to himself. Then a blood-curdling peel of laughter erupted from his throat like a banshee in the sky.

The Bagman stood straight, gripping the ice-pick by the handle and pulled hard. The canvass tore. His foot slipped, and he fell on his butt, sitting on top of the balloon. He twisted his legs and stood back up, still laughing the entire time.

He wedged the pick under the fabric and yanked again. The canvass tore a good three feet.

Mac stood spread legged, peaked on top of the airship like he was riding it and steering with the pick axe. Except, of course, as usual, he was backward.

He yanked again. The pick caught on a piece of thin chain-link reinforcing the balloon. The Bagman inhaled strongly, laughed, and tore through it. The rip in the canvass extended to about eight feet. Room enough for a man to climb in.

Except the madman was laughing so hard, it was evident he was having trouble catching his breath. He almost stopped to spit on the palms of his hands, before he centered himself again, clutching the handle of the pick like he was pulling roots out of the ground.

He leaned backward, his feet sinking into the canvass gasbag, looking up at the sky again, still giggling. He stared upward a moment, then looked down at the fairgrounds. They hadn't reached the beach yet. They were at its edge, but still over Lake Michigan. Somebody might just get out of this thing alive.

He inhaled deeply, guffawed and this time he shook his fist.

"Top o' the world, Ma! To-o-o-p o' the wo-o-orld!" The Bagman yanked hard, turning around, and running toward the front of the ship. Slipping, he almost lost his one-handed grip, but never stopped running. The torn canvass waved behind him like rotten sails in the wind. He fell sideways, bounced himself back up, heels sinking into the balloon up to his ankles.

Canvass ripped like newspaper with every long stroke. The madman just kept digging in, plowing for the front of the ship like a racing horse in the mud. Pitched on the uppermost front of the blimp, the balloon's skin still held pressure. He closed his eyes, gripped the handle hard, and sprinted.

It was like he'd pulled on a zipper. Running hard, every step shoving, until he hit the steep incline of the airship's nose and began to slide, his right hand fixed to the axe-handle, his other in the air like he was riding a bronco. At the last moment, still sliding, the Bagman turned over on his belly. He'd cut thirty yards of the gasbag's canvass, and the middle of the ship was sinking. He could barely hear the gunshots firing from the cabin as they mixed with the soul-draining drone of the ship's engines. The crew was panicking. Something made a cracking sound. Then something broke.

Then the whole ship fell in.

Mac's hand slipped from the axe handle, along with any hope for staying alive. His fingernails dug into the canvass, looking for a seam. Then he realized the hopelessness of the situation. The balloon looked more like a punctured football than an airship.

Another *crack!* And both ends of the ship folded in on the middle.

Bent around the around the vehicle's nosecone, the masked man catapulted up and out like a Human Cannonball. The image flashed across Mac's mind for just an instant, but he could only remember one part of the act; the Human Cannonball had a net.

He was dead. He knew it.

Whirling in the air, he could see the blimp sinking fast beneath him. Men leapt from the cabin as the scrap metal fell around them; every man and molecule spinning in the air, hurtling toward the lake. One of the ship's crew bailed out of the gondola. The crewman's chute barely came out of the pack, before his corpse slapped the ground and flattened on the beach.

The Bagman, who'd just reached the apex of his flight, wondered why he had to be the one to fall the farthest.

He turned himself in the air without thinking. If he was going to die, he'd watch it coming. He wasn't aware he was doing it at the best possible time, while the only wind resistance he would have to deal with was the breeze off the lake. Spread eagled, he hung there, then began to plummet.

Whatever spirit had broken him into hysteria left. He wasn't laughing now. He wasn't even aware of how fast he was falling until his cheeks started slapping around in the wind. He closed his mouth, and realized somebody had stopped screaming.

The crowd outside the Federal Building below pointed at the sky above, unaware they should have been rushing for the exits only seconds before. With the ship safely over the lake, the only thing aimed at them was Mac. He tried swimming in the air again, but it was no good. He grabbed the bottom of his suit's coattail, trying to improvise some wings. The back of his jacket ripped straight up the middle. Reverting to the spread eagle, he clutched at the air trying to aim himself at the Midway. Like a bullet.

Pulling his left arm in, his body rolled and curved in the atmosphere. He lost his balance and spun in circles before he could right himself again. Then he realized there was no way he could grab onto the Sky Ride without being torn limb from limb. Even if he managed to slow himself down he'd still be five stories in the air.

The blurred Midway rushing toward him, he glanced something in his peripheral vision. The Parachute Ride.

His only chance was to grab a silk chute, and hope it would hold together long enough to break his fall. It was coming up fast. Mac flapped his arms. A hundred yards away, at a million miles an hour, he was aimed right at it.

Then he saw the cables.

Aiming himself at the Parachute ride was the stupidest thing he could've done. The odds of catching a silken chute from his height and speed were a million to one. The odds on getting cut in half by one of the cables holding up the chutes were about fifty-fifty. He almost slapped himself in the head before he pulled his arms and legs in, just missing the easternmost parachute wires.

His thigh hit one of the other cables, tearing flesh, and slinging him back toward the Federal Building. Cartwheeling through the air, and falling too fast to make any difference, he spread his arms again, flipped over a few times and righted himself.

The mast of the The City of New York, Admiral Byrd's arctic exploring ship, suddenly stood out and threw itself at him. He pulled his arms in tight and got his feet in front of him, pointing toward the path of his flight like an arrowhead as he dodged by the mast. Whatever he hit, he'd hit feet first. At this rate it wouldn't make any difference.

He was going to die.

Chapter 11
DROWN AND OUT

Ship? Mac thought. *Yeah, a ship, Einstein!*

The force of his fall punched all the air out of him, and a gallon of water went up his nose. That big black spot on the ground had been the lagoon.

Then he was drowning.

Gasping for breath, he spun beneath the water. He'd managed to hit the surface right, but once he'd hit, he'd bent his hips. The result sent him somersaulting under the water feet first. He choked and inhaled a lungful of water.

At least I'll have a body to recover now, he thought, battling for consciousness. Something slammed into the side of his head. He bit down hard on his lip to keep from passing out, spinning, still spinning in the watery tomb. Opening his eyes, all he saw was murk. Thoughts racing, he tried to focus.

He couldn't breathe. He couldn't tell which way was up.

Miniature bubbles from hitting the water tickled the hair on his arms, then his whole body. He wanted to inhale, his chest exploding. Wanting nothing more than to thrash his way out, he forced himself to hang there, in the depths, motionless.

And the bubbles began to rise.

Hands like sledgehammers opened at the end of brawny arms. His feet kicked but it was like swimming in the mud.

He kicked harder, arms extending, pulling at the muck. Tiny blurred lights laughed at him from above. His body tried to inhale again. As hard as he flailed, he simply hung there. All he could see was the light above him.

Two feet below the surface, his mouth opened. To keep from drawing in more water, he forced himself to exhale. Nothing came out. His guts ached. His arms and legs throttled at the quicksand around him. Then everything went black. But he could still see the light.

He wanted to go toward the light.

He blacked out.

Sound rushed at his ears as his head bobbed to the surface. Whiteout. Blackout. He prayed he wouldn't drown now.

His head went back under and both arms circled him, treading water. He bobbed back up and felt the warm summer breeze on his face. Trying to roll over on his back just in case, he simply rolled over. Slowly, his head turned sideways and Mac broke into a perfect Australian crawl. A slow, dead crawl.

His feet hit the silt at the water's edge. As it flowed into his shoes, he didn't have the strength to stand up. He fell face down, and crawled out of the lagoon covered in mud and algae. He looked more like a waterlogged rat than a man as he slid out of the muck, not even realizing his hands were still churning at the ground before him as if he was still in the water. One hand extended into a row of shrubbery that kept passersby out of the lagoon. A soggy, ripped mess of fiber and sludge, dripping in the dirt, dragged itself beneath the bush.

When he passed out he was still clawing at the ground.

Something crawled into his ear, and he woke up. His finger swabbed at whatever it was, and when he opened his eyes he was looking at half a slug on his hand.

"Another beautiful stinkin' day," he mumbled, spitting the mud out of his mouth. Rolling over on his back and looking around, he cursed at the lights.

He'd gotten lucky. Again.

Not just lucky to still be alive, but he'd wound up laying in a row of hedges. Somebody might have seen his leg sticking out or something, but the cops were busy, and everybody else probably thought he was just a drunk sleeping it off.

His leg. He remembered peeling part of it off on the parachute ride cables. Sitting up and grasping his thigh in his hand, he flinched. Through the tear in his slacks he could see the bloody road rash. He was glad he'd at least bounced off the thing instead of peeling by.

Still, the abrasion on his leg felt like somebody had tried to skin him. If he stopped to think about it, he wouldn't be able to walk.

And thinking was his biggest problem right now. Mac's normally scattered brains were scrambled. He moved the rest of his body one part at a time. They all hurt, but seemed to be functioning. Where there's pain there's life.

"I'm full of life," he said, tearing off what was left of his jacket. His shirt came with it. He still had his shoulder holster on, but he'd lost his gun. One leg of his pants was torn off. He felt his face and realized he'd lost his mask in the water.

Putting one hand behind him, he tried to push himself up. He fell back down, but made it on the second attempt. Standing in the middle of the hedgerow, the bushes holding him up, he tried to figure it all out while he wobbled in wind.

Steering himself around, using the hedge branches for handles, he stared blankly across the lagoon. The Federal and State Buildings gradually came into focus. A gray mass of people stood outside, but the rest were all filing back in. The sky ride was above him. He knew where his feet were now, and he moved them. The sediment from the lake in his shoes didn't help. He turned back around and stared into space, not even noticing the passersby, many of whom held their noses up or turned their heads so they wouldn't have to look at such a disturbing figure.

"Hey, mister! The freak show's on the Midway!" said an adolescent voice.

Mac growled, stepped out of the bushes, and the pathway cleared. The kid was right, if he didn't want to draw any attention to himself the Midway would be the best place right now. He stumbled off the sidewalk, finding the shadows, sticking close to buildings and hedges in an effort to make less of a spectacle of himself. His sodden feet slapped the ground, trudging in a death march toward the Rollercoaster.

At the edge of the plaza, he spotted the phone he'd suggested to Crankshaft they use as a communications base. Crankshaft wasn't there, and somebody had torn the mouthpiece off of it. He stepped out of the shadows and kept trudging.

The crowd gave the strange man room as he strode dead-faced across the lawn. Adults noticed and pretended not to; the children were less forgiving. A small gang of kids followed, pointing and trying not to laugh so loudly that the beast might turn and growl again. Mac stumbled and noticed the short-stuff gang behind him. Phrases like "Wassamatter wit' him?" and "Who's da weirdo?" crawled into his ears, only to register in his brain a minute later. The tiny gang grew larger around the edges.

He hung a hard right, and steered himself toward the loading dock of a restaurant. What felt like a hard run, was in reality more like a man stumbling and trying to get his feet in front of himself in time.

The dock resembled a dead end alley, if he could make the service entrance maybe he could find a place to hide. A single bulb in a tin backed reflector was the only brightness. Mac staggered toward the dark corner, praying for the service entrance. But with the steps in front of him, he couldn't raise his leg. Beads of sweat gathered with the dirt and mud on his face. He simply couldn't step that high.

His back hit the wall beside him and he slid down, sitting on the concrete. The kids laughed and pushed each other toward him. The ones that got pushed, scared of the freak, turned and shoved their way back to the center of the gang. Slowly, but still at a distance, they began to encircle him like cockroaches waiting for a sick animal to die. He was hopeless. Probably about to be rolled by a bunch of ten year olds.

Gradually, a tough-looking kid in a sport shirt and a beanie edged toward the beaten man. After daring to come close, one of his hands cautiously reached into Mac's pocket.

A .45 automatic ratcheted theatrically from the shadows of the loading dock behind him. A voice cut through the air.

"Back off, jughead! I know a florist that would be more than happy to sell something to your parents." The voice belonged to Crankshaft.

The adolescent in the beanie jumped backward and tilted his head sideways trying to understand what the ace mechanic had said.

"Funeral wreaths, kid! I'm going to shoot you!"

The cockroaches scattered.

"That was you that went in the lagoon, huh," Crankshaft said shoving the .45 back into his pocket. "I thought you might still be on the plane. Or dead."

"I'm dead. I have to be." Mac spat through broken lips. "And I must be in hell… because you're here."

Crankshaft grabbed him by the wrist and wrapped Mac's arm around his shoulder, helping him to stand. Mac looked at him a moment, then his eyes started staring into space.

"Crank," he said, as if he'd just noticed him. The edges of his lips climbed his face, but it hurt, and he went back to frowning.

Crankshaft felt a kind of pride that Mac had cared enough to insult him even on the edge of consciousness. "C'mon, I'm taking you to the first aid station."

It sounded like Mac said, "I need clothes."

"Doctor doesn't care how you're dressed," Crankshaft said. But he took his jacket off and wrapped it around Mac, before he began dragging him in the direction of the Midway where the first aid station was. They stayed on the grass, until they hit the wide open sawdust where the ticket booths for the rides stood.

"Midway, Crank. Good. I have to get to the Midway," Mac burbled.

"Mac, that was just a kid razzing you."

"No, something's been pulling me toward The Midway all night." Mac clutched Crankshaft's shoulder and began to pull him back toward the shadows next to the public washroom. "Like I'm supposed to be there."

"Because you have to go to the bathroom. You haven't stopped running around for the last four hours."

"I think I went in the lagoon, if you're worried about that," Mac said, still leaning on Crankshaft's shoulder. "It's something else."

"Sally Rand's Balloon Dance?" Crank said, his eyes checking what was left of Mac's pants for stains. He put an arm back under Mac's and steered toward a bench. Strangely enough, on The Midway people didn't seem to notice them yet. At least nobody had started screaming that the Sideshow Geek had broken out of his cage.

Crank pushed Mac down on the bench, and craned his neck checking out the crowd, and trying to figure out how to keep Mac from drawing their attention. Mac sat back with his eyes closed a moment.

Crankshaft, thinking Mac had passed out again, slapped him back and forth across the cheek. Mac caught the ace mechanic's wrist in motion and opened his opened his eyes.

"Damnit, Crank. I'm awake. I just need to rest, take some time, walk this thing off..." His eyelids were heavy.

"Mac, you moron, this isn't a sport! You just fell a half-mile out of the sky!"

Mac opened one eye, and started to grin.

The moon spread over the heavens. The lights of the Worlds Fair reflected off the lagoon. Strollers and baby carriages followed the route to the boardwalk, while others came off the beach headed in the other direction. Beneath the roar of the .22 rifles in the shooting galleries, the tin pan sounds of merry-go-rounds and the buzzing attractions their voices could barely be heard. Bells, whistles and gongs mixed with the din of the rollercoaster, the hawkers, and the crowd.

Turning his head toward Crankshaft, Mac twitched, and looked back in the other direction. Suddenly, his eyes went wide, and the man who had looked like a broken down geek only a moment before, jolted upright in his seat. His eyebrows shifted down to hang malevolently over his eyes, and the edges of his mouth went up like a carnivore showing off its fangs.

Crankshaft had been too busy calling Mac names to notice, until the barrel-chested, big man jumped out of his seat. Crank could see he was chewing on his tongue, his hands curled into fists at his side, his whole body flexed. At first it reminded him of a wind-up toy, getting ready to take a step, then he realized it was more like watching a hunting dog catching a scent.

Mac just stood there. Staring and flexing.

A hundred yards away from them, past an alley full of games of chance, just beyond the people throwing baseballs at milk bottles with weighted bottoms, stood a lad in Eastern European styled lederhosen. He was standing between two tents, and he was still smiling. The boy held Mac's wallet in the air, and waved a finger at him.

The big man exploded. Mac snarled and broke into an urgent stride, ignoring the pain in his body. Crankshaft, surprised, jumped up to follow. Across the sawdust lot, the boy started laughing.

Mac sprinted by the games of chance, and crossed into the aisle next to the freak show where a row of tiny sideshow tents lay closer to the lake. The boy broke into a run, and sprinted down the narrow line of tents.

Mac and Crankshaft circled from the other side and cut him off. The little gypsy thief halted in front of an even slimmer red tent, decorated in fine gold brocade that made it stand out from the others. His eyes met those of his hunters. His feet shifted in two different directions. Then he ducked inside the strangely decorated sideshow.

Without thought, Mac flew up the path, swept the tent flaps out of his way and stepped inside.

Behind a table in the center of the tent, a gnarled old woman sat with a deck of cards and a bowl of water in front of her. The boy slapped the wallet on the table and stood behind the old crone, wagging his head and shrugging his shoulders. Mac could tell he was trying not to giggle. The big man took a step forward, his arms extended to grab the brat before he could get away. But something stopped him.

Two gargantuan men wielding curved swords stepped out of the shadows behind the old woman. Men who looked more like seventeenth century warriors than carnival workers. Mac spun around and saw two more behind him. Both wore wool tunics, round hats and long pants, but their suspenders matched the gypsy boy's. The medieval guards gripped the handle of their blades with both hands, blocking the entrance to the tent with four wide inches of steel apiece.

Mac's eyes and mouth, his whole face, clenched like he'd just seen a car wreck. His body shook, before he felt every square inch of its pain. They'd been expecting him. *It was a trap.*

"Look at him," the old woman said. "Is he not beautiful?"

...the boy held Mac's wallet in the air...

Chapter 12
THE PROPHECY

Mac eyes went up and down his body. *Beautiul?* He was bruised, bloody, shirtless, and what was left of his pants was falling down. His coppery brown hair stuck straight up and was covered in mud. He exhaled like he was deflating.

"Lady, you should see me after a trip to the barber shop."

He glanced to get a better look at the guards by the door, and accidentally staggered. They had fifty pounds on him apiece, all muscle, and they were in a lot better shape. He noticed the tent flaps wave behind the guards, and both men's broad blades blocking the entrance.

Damnit! Mac mentally cursed himself. He'd forgotten Crankshaft was walking into the same trap.

The old woman nodded, and the men returned their swords to their scabbards to let the next victim in.

Crankshaft took two steps inside, stopped behind Mac and reached for his .45. The point of a cold, steel dagger pressed into his side like a message. Crankshaft got the message, and slowly pulled his gun out between thumb and forefinger. He held it out and away from himself like a hypochondriac avoiding germs before he dropped it. The automatic hit the sawdust with a thump.

With no physical means of escape, Mac tried to think of a way out. Normally, in a situation like this his thoughts would be ricocheting around inside his head like pinballs, but instead, he had nothing. He was tired, confused, beat up and he still couldn't think straight.

But thinking straight wasn't Mac's strong point anyway. No, forget that. There was only one thing to do in this situation and it was something Mac had mastered back when he'd just been a kid grifting for food. *Keep your game face on, and keep talking.*

Mac glanced over his shoulder at Crankshaft. The jaded mechanic nodded back. To an onlooker it would seem like they had agreed on a plan. But the onlooker would have been fooling themselves because that nod meant be ready for anything.

Mac was an ex-criminal who knew there was no such thing as a perfect plan. His first rule had always been: improvise. Crankshaft Jones was a veteran of the hardest fighting combat unit of the entire World War. He knew how to kill or be killed. Between the two of them, they were quick, clever, and deadly when they had to be. Mac kept telling himself this as he acknowledged the pain of the beating he'd taken. Then he concentrated on dealing with the situation at hand.

The big man in torn pants smiled, grabbed the back of the wooden chair in front of the table, spun it around and smiled. He sat down spread legged and folded his arms across the back of the chair.

"Who are you? And what do you want?"

The old crone smiled without parting her lips, spread her arms and looked at each of the guards. She must have inhaled deeply, because she exhaled and smiled more, looking up at the ceiling of a tent that had traveled from the Black Forest. She inhaled as if she were about to speak, but didn't. Instead, she fanned a deck of 6" X 3" cards across the dark, scarred wood, and rested her palms on the edge of the table.

"Pick a card."

Mac's eyelids were at half mast, but an evil gleam ignited in the eyes beneath them. "Any card?"

"It's very simple," the old woman said. She wasn't smiling anymore.

"Lady, I know this trick."

She made a presentation of looking him over, up and down. "It is quite obvious you do not."

Mac glanced over his shoulder at Crankshaft again.

"Take a card. It's the fortune of a lifetime," she said with no expression whatsoever. There was something about the old woman. Her presence could have filled the big top, and yet she seemed no more than a bag of bones wrapped in a parchment paper skin.

Mac reached out and turned a card over. The card depicted a man in armor riding a horse, with the reins in one hand, and a golden goblet clutched in the other.

"Do you know the meaning of this card?" The old woman's eyes burned into Mac's. Mac didn't flinch.

"Yeah. It means you want five bucks, then you string me along for more, till I'm outta' money," he said. "I drew the card. Who are you?"

"My name is Mirella Herne. I'm a traveler." Without batting an eye she collected the cards back into her hand with one swoop, and then reached into the shadows behind her. She placed a second deck of big cards on the table and said, "Pick another."

"'Traveler,' that's just a fancy name for Gypsy, right?" Mac turned over a second card.

Again, the card revealed a knight astride a horse with a goblet clutched in his hand. Mac grappled at the cards, flipping them over in batches. There were no other cards with the knight and the horse on them. It wasn't a trick deck. The old woman looked at the guards and smiled impishly. She grabbed a ten inch high stack of cards along with the ones on the table, threw them all in the air and giggled.

The cards roiled and twisted, dancing as they fell to the floor. All of them. Not one card landed on the table, or the bowl of water that sat upon it. Not one card rested on the benches or single stools in the corners. Not one had touched the guards or even dropped across one of their boots.

Mac's mouth fell a little open. It was like the cards had been shot out of a machine. He glanced under the table looking for a magician's card cannon. There wasn't even a tablecloth to conceal it; if that had that been the case.

Without moving from his seat, Mac reached down and peeled a card off the floor to his right. It was the same card with the knight, the horse, and the cup on it. Behind him, Crankshaft flipped over some cards with his toes. They were all different. If nothing else, the lady was a hell of a card dealer.

Another deck of cards appeared in Mirella Herne's hand, and the old woman spoke in a soothing voice, yet one that crackled with fire.

"Mr. McCullough, that card is called 'The Knight of Cups.' You might be lucky enough to draw another if you wish. But, for the most part, you will always draw The Knight of Cups."

"Waitaminnit!" Mac said. He wasn't aware of it, but he'd completely forgotten about his bruises and abrasions. "First, I'm not amazed that you know my name; you stole my wallet!"

"It was the only way to bring you here," she said.

"Bring me... here?"

"We were destined to meet you here. You cannot see your own aura, can you?"

Mac didn't bother to glance. He looked at Crankshaft and slapped his knee. Crankshaft's head rolled with his eyes as he stepped into the lantern light.

"I knew a dancer once named Destiny Aura," Crankshaft said, elbowing Mac in the shoulder.

The two guards inside the front entrance, grabbed Crankshafts shoulders from behind, picked him up in the air and sat him down between them. They looked at the ace mechanic like he should know better. Crank gave them the stink-eye right back.

"This is no time for levity, Mr. McCullough. The world will be a very tough place for you if you never find out what you are."

"Mir, the world *is* a tough place." Mac crossed his arms over the back of the chair again.

"And yet, you always seem to just slide by. Am I right?"

"What do you mean?" Mac leaned forward in his seat.

"You are not necessarily a bad man, are you, Mr. McCullough?"

Mac scratched his head for a moment, pulled a slice of dry mud off his scalp, and threw it on the floor. "Not necessarily."

Mirella laughed. It was actually kind of charming, like something you might hear in a doily-filled Russian Tearoom. The old woman smiled at everyone in the tent. The boy pickpocket, who had never stopped smiling, waved and let himself out of the flaps behind her. Five of the seven people left in the tent seemed warm and comfortable.

"You are not necessarily a good man, either. Are you, Mr. McCullough?"

"Morality doesn't change. Ethics can be modified. The world is complicated, too," Mac answered. "Now, how about you answer some of my questions?"

"More will be revealed, Mr. McCullough. It is the way of life. You needn't worry." She pulled a small clay pitcher out of the firmament and placed it on the table. "Watch." The old crone poured more water into the bowl.

"I'm not drinking that," Mac said. "Speaking of which, anybody got a cigarette that's not laced with cyanide or some kinda' mojo?"

One or two of the guards, it was hard to tell they were so big, threw a brand Mac had never seen before on the table.

"It's Turkish," one of them said, leaning over Mac.

Mac popped two smokes out of the top of the pack, and aimed it at the guard. The guard looked at Mirella. She gave him a nod. The guard took the cigarette, lit it, and then gave Mac the pack of matches. Mac waited a few puffs, to see if the man keeled over. Then lit up, inhaled, exhaled, and sighed. Crankshaft took a slug of bootleg corn liquor from his flask, and sat it on the table next to Mac.

Mirella swept the liquor from the table with a wave of her arm. "That will only make your pain worse. I've sent the boy for some tea."

The moment the sound of her voice stopped, the tiny Gypsy pickpocket swept through the flaps, and between the two guards stationed behind the old woman. He was carrying a platter with a teapot and several large cups on it. He placed the platter in the darkness behind her, bowed, and disappeared once again.

"The same kid who stole his wallet," Crankshaft added, picking up his flask from the floor, happy he hadn't left the lid unscrewed. "Lady, in any other situation you might almost make sense. Hell, I think you could even be a nice person but…"

"It's very good tea, Mr.….? Antoine Jones, is it?"

"Yes, it is." Crankshaft barely used his real name anymore. Mac hadn't even known it till a few months ago.

The aforesaid Mr. McCullough was puffing on his cigarette like it was oxygen, and secretly waving his arm around behind his back trying to get Crankshaft to slip him the whiskey flask. Crankshaft put the flask in his own pocket, and gave the Gypsy woman the same nod she'd given her guards. A willing respect.

Mirella Herne shoved the wooden bowl of water into the center of the table, directly in front of Mac. She sprinkled powder from one hand and pepper from the other over the bowl. The black and white powders swirled in the water as if they were running away from each other. Then, gradually, shapes began to form, twisting and changing as if the powders had created transmutable works of print, visions of the unseen.

Mac eyed the bowl suspiciously.

An image of a young boy, and two policemen appeared in the bowl.

"Mr. McCullough, you were orphaned even as you reached manhood, or quite possibly abandoned. You are a thief…"

Mac's back straightened as if he'd been insulted, but a picture of him appeared in the bowl. In the image, Mac parked one truck next to another that looked just like it, then climbed into the second truck and drove off; effectively hijacking one vehicle and substituting a decoy. Something he'd done some ten years before. Mirella Herne continued.

"But you are a thief who sees himself in others. You rarely steal from the weak and infirm, but choose to go after the powerful…"

"That's where the money is," Mac said. Mirella looked up from beneath her eyebrows as if he'd intruded.

"You have a sense of humor…"

Mac opened his mouth to say something.

"…of sorts," she interrupted. "Take note, in the old world the word 'humor' is also used to describe moodiness. These moods make you a thief with a certain… morality, or ethics if you will. You are not afraid of work, but care more about freedom than money. You have hidden talents, performing feats in wide-ranging fields that professionals would envy."

"Jack of all trades, master of none," Crankshaft muttered.

"You have a friend who aids you with weapons, rather than a squire or paid help." Mirella smiled at Crankshaft, then looked directly back into Mac's puffy eyes. "You were forced recently to travel from the East to the West."

A vision of Mac from less than two years ago eddied across the water in the strange wooden bowl. He was slipping out of the back of a four-star hotel, peeling off a coat and mustache, and flagging down a cab as the house detective missed him by less than two minutes. A crowd of people in evening dress rushed from the front desk of the hotel to the street beyond, looking for the man who'd just promised to make them rich. Of course, all that was left of that character was the coat and mustache.

"I left Philadelphia!" Mac's palms turned up in his lap, shoulders shrugging an excuse. Mirella didn't let him finish.

"You have recently donned a mask, so that evil people won't know you do good."

Mac looked over at Crankshaft. The two of them twisted from the waist up, heads nodding around, making odd gestures but not one of the moves was a definite yes or no.

"What do you want, lady?" Mac stood up, stopping just short of pushing the chair over. He turned and eyed the massive guards as they loosened their swords in their scabbards. He looked back at Mirella Verne with pleading eyes.

"I have but a few questions more, and you should know all," she said. "Besides, I believe you need to learn the difference between patience and perseverance." She almost winked at him. "Mr. McCullough, are you given to trance states?"

"Like I've been hypnotized? I don't think so," he said, in a tone that made clear the answer was 'no.'

"He sleepwalks." Crankshaft stepped from out from the shadows between the guards. Nobody tried to stop him this time. "At least that's what we were thinking it might be. I've seen him do it three times. It's like he's hung over or something, sits and stares for days at a time. Sometimes stops to write in a notebook. Comes back next day, knowing things I don't think *he* understands."

The room was silent for a while. Mirella Verne picked up the bowl of water and slung it in the sawdust behind her. With no wasted motion, her hands came back to the table grasping the teapot and several cups stacked inside each other.

Mac sat back down. The guards stared stoically ahead the entire time, while the old woman traded an assuring glance for Mac and Crankshaft's ominous looks. She poured herself a cup of tea and leaned back in her chair.

"Mr. McCullough, you are not just any thief." She pointed at him, and with something akin to awe in her voice said, "You *are* The Knight of Cups; The King of Thieves!"

Chapter 13
HOLY KNIGHT!

"The night of cups?" Mac said, staring at the tea set on the table in front of him. "I don't get it."

Crankshaft slapped him on the side of the head with his flat cap. "Not the tea cups, Mac. Like on the tarot deck, the cards, the knight with the horse and the cup."

Mac looked at the tarot card he'd pulled off the floor. "I still don't get it."

Mirella poured two more cups of tea, and placed them where the men could reach them.

"Pull up a stool, Mr. Jones. You are a part of this too."

Crankshaft did so and sat down to sip his tea. Mac still eyed his warily.

"Drink the tea, Mr. McCullough. You will be surprised," she said. "It is rejuvenating in a sense that most tea is not. I am a lot older than I look."

Mac thought about saying that was impossible, but, upon looking at the ancient fortune teller, found he couldn't. He sipped his tea. It was strong and spicy, and burned his tongue.

"Are either of you gentleman familiar with the legend of The Fourth Nail?"

Both men shook their heads *no*.

"It is written that when Jesus Christ was crucified, the Romans used four nails to hang him on the cross. A passing traveler, a Gypsy, upon seeing Jesus' pain, stole that fourth nail. And for that reason alone, the Gypsy's were given the right to steal with the Lord's blessing."

"Oh, *that* fourth nail. Well, I have heard the legend, but I'm pretty sure the local District Attorney doesn't take 'what is written' too seriously, Mirella." Mac put his teacup on the table. He wanted more. "No more offense meant but wouldn't that legend actually make him King of the Gypsies and thieves and lawyers and bankers and all that?"

"It is all linked, Mr. McCullough. More will be revealed." Mirella refilled Mac's cup from the teapot. "Yes, that man was to become King of the Gypsies, but he was one in a hundred. You see, sirs, even among Gypsies, there are still secrets."

Mac turned the card around in his hand looking for them. Mirella's lips set hard, but her eyes drifted far away as she spoke.

"The cards in the tarot are older than the Gypsies, the Romans, even the Babylonians; farther than recorded time. While cards have changed illustrations over the years, the ancient meanings are collected from tales either true or moral. While the depiction of the man in armor..." Her eyes focused on Mac again. "...the knight on *your* card came much later, after the crusades. Obviously, due to European social standards, the current picture represents a Knight in King's service. One who seeks the Holy Grail."

Mac's eyebrows knitted down on his forehead. Crankshaft leaned back from the waist up like he was waiting for a cobra to strike.

"You are not that man," Mirella finished.

Both The Bagman and ace mechanic exhaled the breath they'd been holding.

"But, take warning!" Mirella almost whispered, "The symbol of the Holy Grail is an apt metaphor for the man who draws The Knight of Cups and especially, for the man who *is* The Knight of Cups. Much like the Knights of the Round Table seeking the grail, the Knight of Cups is on a great mission or quest. But that great mission may very well kill him.

"Now, I need you to understand that the first King of the Gypsies was a Knight of Cups but not all Knights of Cups are Gypsies." Mirella waved her hand over the table and turned it over slowly into a fist. "Many, however, are thieves." Her words hung in the air.

"So...? I'm supposed to be a thief?" Mac's eyebrows raised and his mouth turned to one side.

"Not necessarily."

"A hero?" Mac queried, beginning to turn his head sideways.

Mirella Verne's hand shot from behind the table like she was going to slap him. Instead, she held his jaw in her palm, her fingers clasping the cabled muscles on his neck. "You will *have to* be a hero."

"Whoa, now waitaminnit," Mac started to ramble, "I don't have to be anything. That's been my motto up till now, and it's been working just fine!"

Mirella, Crankshaft, even the heavily muscled guards, eyed Mac sitting straddle-legged, backwards in his chair. His hair sticking up caked in mud. Cuts, bruises and abrasions tattooed his flesh. With no shirt on, the welts across his chest from the shoulder holster looked like third degree burns. His left pant leg was torn, the right one missing, both displaying fallen socks, and shoes a little less muddy than the rest of him.

"Yes, you are doing wonderful, Mr. McCullough." Mirella continued to pour from her bottomless teapot. "You will *have* to be hero, because of who you are. The Knight of Cups is both a blessing and a curse, yin and yang if you prefer, for while he may have a license to steal, he does not have license to do evil. Whatever he does, whatever you do, Mr. McCullough, boomerangs back at you. If it is ultimately good, you will be rewarded. If it is bad, you will be destroyed. Although, from observation, I can tell it is one of the lessons you're already learning. It is a lesson in balance."

"Boy, have you got the wrong guy," Mac said. "Listen, I appreciate the tea and all, but why me?"

"Almost two-thousand years ago, Mr. McCullough, one of my relatives was there to see that King of Thieves remove the fourth nail from the crucifixion. Since then, it has been the job of my family and ancestors, many long since forgotten, to find and enlighten the newest Knights. Once in a lifetime a Knight of Cups is born. Once in a lifetime a King of Thieves is born. You are both of those men. And now that I have told you so, I can face death with contentment in my heart."

Mac's eyes shifted on everybody in the room distrustfully. He wanted to believe it but he'd grown up in the company of con men and pickpockets, and it was quite evident that Mirella's crew ran in the same direction. Mac hated the dilemma of trust among thieves; it had plagued him since childhood. How do you trust the people that taught you to trust nobody?

Crankshaft seemed to believe it, but was it because he wanted to? Who wouldn't want to be a "weapons master?" Well, Mac for one. He used guns because he had to, not because he wanted to.

That was the problem. Everything fit.

Mirella's Gypsies weren't telling fortunes and reading palms with the other Gypsies on the Midway. They'd stationed themselves almost in the background, by the fence away from the crowd. There wasn't even a sign on the front of the tent. They had come here expressly for him.

The wooden bowl that projected pictures, better than the television in the Science Building, real life pictures, of real things no one had ever seen? Sure, it looked like it was beyond science, but a lot of science looks like magic. No, nobody had seen some of the stuff the old broad had showed them. A lot of it, Mac hadn't exactly been ready to brag about to begin with. Yet it was there.

That card trick with the decks exploding from the table? Mac had sifted through the cards. If there was a trick, he wasn't in on it.

Crankshaft's full name, Mac's sleepwalking and the so-called trance state, the kid even knowing whose wallet to steal to begin with. All of it was too real.

Hell, if they'd really wanted to hurt him, the guards could have killed him already. Mac still kept coming up with the same question: *Even if it's real, what am I supposed to do?*

Almost as if she'd read his mind, the old gypsy fortune teller, for that's what Mac had decided Mirella Verne was for real, continued to speak.

"You have more power than you know, Mr. McCullough. I believe tonight may be a test. All you have to do is the right thing."

"How will I know what the right thing is?"

"You've always known. This whole time you've been confused trying to help both yourself and others. You can only guarantee your safety by help-ing others."

"What, no *quid pro quo* for the kid?" Crankshaft had always considered The Bagman a for-profit entity.

Miranda gave him a pleasant nod, and while she didn't exactly smile, her mouth curved up at the edges. "As long as others profit, I believe you'll be allowed to do the same."

"Mirella, I don't want to seem ungrateful or anything, but what about hurting people?" Mac lit another cigarette, and poured himself a cup of tea. "We can debate the difference between ethics and morality all day, but there are people running this toddling town that don't even know the meaning of the words."

"To protect others, it is no problem." Mirella realized she had gained Mac's trust when he started pouring his own tea. "Kings and Knights do the same. Remember, you are both."

Mac stared at Mirella a moment, then Crankshaft. He told himself if something was too good to be true, then it was probably a con. That was a fact of life. He puffed on his cigarette a few more times, extinguished it between his fingers and dropped the butt into the sawdust. He downed the cup of tea and put it back on the table. If he was going to reject them, he better be polite about it.

Then, even as he put the teacup back on the table, his other hand fell onto his thigh. It stung, but he had touched it without wanting to scream. Thinking he better get an icepack on the wound quick, or the swelling would put him out of action, he took inventory of the abrasion.

Even there in the light of a single lantern, what should have been a red and black bruised mess was kind of pink. Gently touching his palm to his leg, he realized it stung, but like a bruise, like some kid had hit him with a baseball. Then he realized he felt the hairs on his leg, where just a few minutes ago had been a four-inch wide scab.

It hit him like a hammer. When the old broad had said the tea was rejuvenating, she hadn't been kidding. No, Mac had seen a lot of cons, but Mirella Verne wasn't one of them.

He turned to look back at Mirella and say *yes*. She cut him off.

"Mr. Jones, since it seems our new knight must run the gauntlet this evening, I'm going to leave this bit of information with you." She handed Crankshaft a sheaf of folded documents. "Also, there is a phone number and address on there, so that you may contact us should you have any questions."

Mac grabbed the papers, checked the address and phone number. It was a street on the edge of Greektown.

"You will not find us there unless you are truly in need, Mr. McCullough."

She held a finger in the air. "And remember, none shall speak for me except for my sons; Ker, Tobar, Belcher and Wesh."

The four muscle-bound guards seemed to impossibly straighten their backs even more and, grinning, gave Mac a salute. The two in the front of the tent stepped forward. The largest of them made a pounding motion with his fist, and smiling, said, "Knock 'em dead, Yankee."

"Ker and Tobar would be chiefs themselves, did they not prefer muscle to stealth," Mirella finished, as the two men stepped back by the entrance.

"I have one other question for you, Mr. McCullough," the fortune teller said.

She had Mac's attention. The one thing Mac didn't like was more responsibility, and it had just been heaped on him. He was convinced if he could just blow this question, he could get out from under her spell.

"What size suit do you wear? About a fourty-four I should guess with that chest of yours."

She was right. Mac didn't say a word as the same kid who'd stolen his wallet slid through the rear flaps of the tent with a navy-blue, three piece suit, shirt and tie, all on one hangar.

"I took the liberty of sending the boy to search some of the employee lockers. I would have hated to send him out again." She said it as if she were discussing a delivery from the milkman.

Mac held the suit in front of him. Ker, Tobar, Belcher and Wesh grabbed wet washcloths from their belts and surrounded the big man. They turned their backs, blocking the view as he washed and changed clothes, and when Mac stepped out of the circle he looked almost like his old self. The suit fit like it was tailored for him.

Mac wondered about a hat.

"Regarding your next question, Mr. McCullough. You'll have to steal a hat of your own, preferably from someone evil. But I do have something else for you." The old woman slung a burlap bag on the table. There was elastic in the neck, and two eyeholes cut into it. "You won't have as much time and trouble holding onto this one."

Mac eyed the coarse material suspiciously.

"A new mask? No, I couldn't... Oooooo, it's so-o-oft," he said, running his fingers inside the bag. "Silk lined?"

It didn't look as sharp as the chamois leather mask Coco had made for him but it was scary looking. Kind of like a western pulp vigilante. Mac would hang onto his old mask, but this one, well, it was *really* soft inside. Mac tucked it into the pocket of the suit, and stood up, unsure what came next.

"Well... uh, thanks, Mirella. We'll be in touch," he said.

"Thank you, Mr. McCullough."

"Call me Mac…" he said, shaking her hand. "…or The Bagman."

As Mac left, the Gypsy woman put something else in Crankshaft's hand, and the two exchanged meaningful nods; Mac was going to need the ace mechanic's help. So it was written, so it should come to pass.

When both men were outside, Mac remembered he had wanted to ask about getting more of Mirella's rejuvenating tea. He turned, flipping open the tent flaps only find the tiny sideshow *yurt* empty. Not even a chair and tables.

The old broad didn't kid around.

Chapter 14
THE COMING OF RESONANCE

Conrad Wilcox was angry. Which wouldn't have been important, except that was *why* Conrad Wilcox was angry. He had never been important.

The son of real estate and investment tycoon Randolph Wilcox, Connie had been raised amid, no, he had studied, the ways of wealth, the intricacies of the finer things in life. They had taught him about privilege.

His family sent him to the best schools and visited on holidays. Yet he understood the reasons for their absence. His dad was busy selling different parts of the world. His mom sailed along with dad, from Europe to Africa to South America. And every year his parents would get back from this trip at about the same time "Little Connie" had to go back to private school.

Randolph, being the manly type, wanted his son to participate in athletic activities. The old man had wanted Conrad on the football or baseball team. But Conrad had never felt the same sense of camaraderie as others on the team, or even at school for that matter.

So instead, he played polo. In fact, young Wilcox learned only from the finest of coaches and had his own team of horses. But he lacked the one thing every good rider has to have. A connection to his horse.

In the evenings, convinced that the maid and butler were spies for his dad, Connie would wait until the house staff was off duty before sneaking out to the night clubs. He didn't drink much there, and he didn't dance much. But Connie listened. He listened to all those *hep* jazz musicians, the tones intertwining melodies from one source to the next. The way flat notes mixed with pure ones, *and how two different sounds could make one big percussive pulse.*

Conrad's father believed music lessons were a waste of time and money. The old man had refused to let him study anything unrelated to the business world. Conrad rebelled by taking piano lessons, but everything he played was creaky and the timing was off. Unfortunately, his father had been right. The young man had a tin ear and didn't even know it.

Again, Conrad had lacked that one thing that all good musicians have to have. He never looked forward to playing some part of a composition he knew. He never savored a musical movement unless he was the one playing it. He had never felt the wonder of other composers, or the camaraderie of the other musicians. And he had never been one with his instrument. He "walked as he dreamed, alone," and separate as if there were a wall between him and the world.

He had been biding his time in school, when he heard about an honors course in Sonics to be taught at the University. Conrad immediately went to the science lab and signed up on the spot.

His goal was simple, though he couldn't tell his father. Conrad wanted to invent an electrical jazz instrument. It was so simple, he liked to remind himself, because he was a man of higher mind. In this brave new age of electricity, Conrad Wilcox would be the first man to create an instrument of harnessed musical lightning.

But, after three years in the Sonics labs, Conrad's studies had gone beyond those of his teachers. While working on his own secret project, an experiment not approved by the Dean of Sciences, Conrad blew the walls off a laboratory, and was expelled immediately. Permanently.

Two days later Léon Theremin patented the world's first electric musical instrument, synonymously named the Theremin. Conrad had lost the race.

Soon he'd almost lost interest in music. But not power.

For other than its power source, Conrad's sonic designs had much less to do with electricity than the Theremin, and more to do with pure amplified Sonics. Conrad's research had been centered in what he called "stereoscopic projection," two amplifiers mixing tones and notes. Amplifiers which aimed the sounds, mixing them separately from one location, and aiming them so that the sonic "beams" would cross nearby. The two musical tones mixed to create a force all its own; a resonant tone that would shake whatever it was aimed at. A sort of sonic short circuit. Like gasoline and fire.

Borrowing money from his father, the younger Wilcox had founded his own company, Wilcox Radio Enterprises, and for four years continued his research. While the company grew, Conrad was able to live off his stock market investments at a time when they couldn't fail. At least that's what people thought.

Then came the Crash of '29.

Not only did Conrad lose his sound and research company, but he had invested heavily in the market on "margin," meaning he was paying for stocks with the same stocks he already owned at a margin of ten-to-one. Needless to say, he couldn't keep paying for failed stocks with his own failed stock.

And he was now a million dollars in debt.

Unable to pay his employees, he salvaged his one remaining project, The Resonance Gun, and rallied everything for a sale to the U.S. Army. But

...two musical tones mixed to create a force...

the government wasn't interested. The technology was too new, untested, and most of all, dangerous.

Then, the fates laughed at Conrad again. His father Randolph Wilcox, also bankrupted in the Crash, committed suicide. Conrad had nothing. No capital, no liquid, no hope and no friends.

But always, always, there were the bill collectors. Forced to hide from his creditors Conrad went underground, living in hotels under assumed names, and later, a shotgun shack by the railroad. Places where he could be alone with his thoughts, his diagrams, and his machines. Solitude soon became isolation.

And Wilcox became a man arguing with his mind.

He had done everything he was supposed to. He had gone to school, he had worked for his own betterment, and he had wasted his *own valuable time* putting up with people shallower and less intelligent than himself. He had played the game. But the game was rigged.

The rich got richer, the poor got the picture. But what about him?

They had pulled the rungs off the ladder to bring him down. The halls of the elite were a wealthy private club now, and upstarts like Conrad weren't allowed. The fools could not see his greatness. Not even his own father.

Given the power of the Resonance Gun and the fragile state of Conrad's mind, it was inevitable that he would take the weapon he couldn't give away and use it himself. The amazing thing was that he took the time to modify it. Conrad was nothing if not a perfectionist, in the things he cared about, and all Conrad cared about was sound and fury.

Thanks to his less than studious past, Conrad still had acquaintances at the polo grounds, the horse tracks, and the betting parlors. One bent criminal sent him to the next, until he'd gathered a small army in a warehouse on the west side, and the men assembled stood before the large, original Resonance Cannon.

With some fifty men listening, Conrad had offered up his plan. At least thirty of the men applauded wildly as they heard it. Some fifteen to twenty weren't interested.

"If you feel you must take your leave," Conrad said, "then, please, take your leave." As men shuffled back and forth, the ones who decided to use the door were held up by Conrad. "Hold on a second…"

The tiny formation by the exit exploded in a cloud of flesh and blood. And Conrad had the beginning of a mob.

They funded themselves through several bank robberies, literally tearing open the vaults with sonic vibration, but the money was still not enough. To impress his future criminal cohorts, Conrad perfected a "silencer" for automatic weapons. And within three months he had completed a battery powered Resonance Gun that would strap to his wrist.

Yes, after a lifetime of privilege, Conrad Wilcox was walking around with a gun up his sleeve. All he had to do was twist a dial and aim. The two different wavelengths would center on the resonant tone of whatever he aimed at and the world would shake.

He liked the idea of shaking the world. Originally he'd planned on plain old extortion and blackmail. Then Conrad had heard about Chicago's attempt at a World Fair.

It was perfect. The world had done him wrong, and he could think of no better place to take his revenge. So much better to have all of them pay, rather than just a few.

He'd planned everything perfectly. Those he couldn't bribe he blackmailed. One time going so far as to threaten the Fair's Personnel Director, and then kidnapping his family. By the time word got out on the street they were missing, he'd killed the personnel director, too. He told no one, not even his "partners." If the kidnap victims had been found it would have killed the plan.

And the plan was everything. Resonance was born for the plan.

It was simple. He'd kill the Romanian Ambassador, for which he would be paid handsomely by a foreign government; something else his newfound "partners" need not know about. The murder would spark an unruly crowd, one that couldn't escape en-masse, because if they rushed the exits they'd be shot. Sure, if everybody made the right decision and stampeded the gates, Resonance's plan didn't stand a chance. But Resonance knew normal people didn't act that way.

Just in case, he made the second killing a little less sensational. That way the crowd would simply mill about, restless but not running. Not yet. No, given the shiny new ball of The World's Fair, the crowd would distract themselves.

Then, while the people herded like cattle in a lightning storm below, he would rain hell down on them. The original Resonant Sound Cannon, mounted inside a small airship disguised as a blimp, its guts loaded with a junkyard full of scrap shrapnel. Thousands would die. The world would shudder at the newfound power of sound. The city would pay, and Resonance would rule as he should.

Again, Conrad told himself, he'd done everything he was supposed to. Success could not elude him. Then this "Bagman" character had shown up. Wilcox had never heard of him, and when he asked one of his henchmen.

"Just a local idiot," was the answer.

Well, the local idiot had put half his team out of commission on their first meeting. With cleaning products! He'd forced Conrad to shave his goatee off so he wouldn't be recognized, and almost delayed his air-tight schedule.

Then the masked pain-in-the-ass discovered the booby-trapped Tele-tractor before anyone else, quashing Resonance's hope to slowly *build* the crowd to a panic. Thanks to the masked man what should have been a staircase of destruction, a musical scale written to rise to the ultimate cre-scendo and eminent glory, was transformed into nothing. Zero! Zilch! The only ones that noticed at all were the cops; the real ones.

This Bagman had ruined his symphony. He'd killed all the melody and left nothing behind but the *sturm* and *drang* of some aboriginal tin-pan al-ley mash. Like Beethoven being played by The Katzenjammer Kids. It was an insult to Resonance, and thus in his mind, to the justice of the world.

The man who had been Conrad Wilcox lowered his binoculars as he stood a half-mile away. He listened as one of his men fell screaming from the blimp in the sky. There was silence. Then he hit the beach with a thud.

Resonance had seen the yellow stunt plane, and thought nothing of it. Just local rubes paying for a plane ride, right? Then he'd heard the radio through a portable receiving device in his ear. First, yelling about the plane diving at them, then, screaming that a man had landed on the balloon; they were going down.

Resonance had watched from the ground as some suicidal fool tore his airship open, from stem to stern with what looked like a pick-axe. It was dark, but he'd seen the tan color of that damned chamois cloth mask.

He had watched as men leapt from the falling blimp's cabin, they're parachutes barely opening, then dragging them beneath the surface of Lake Michigan to a watery death. He lowered his binoculars unable to see after an electric flash from the airships hull. He heard one man scream, falling, until the skydiver hit the cobblestone walkway with a thud. Two of the men had hit the beach. One of them had survived.

Now the Police were all over them. Wilcox had paid off the right people, but not every cop in Chicago was on the take. Word was now officially out that something was wrong at The World's Fair.

Gangs of angry Chicagoans at the 23rd Street entrance attacked Reso-nance's bogus security guards and police. The city police were quick to order a paddy wagon on the scene, where Chicago's finest, finding the cops on the take had already disappeared, demonstrated their patience by ar-resting everybody else.

The Resonance cannon aimed at the State and Federal Buildings was to have been his grand finale, a sweet symphony of death. His orchestration of the killing of thousands would have forced them to take him seriously. He would have been rich. He would have been powerful.

Why would they not let him be somebody? *Why must they always drag me down?*

He hadn't seen what had happened to The Bagman, and assumed he was dead because the man was a fool. But it didn't matter. It was too late. And the man who had been Conrad Wilcox had nothing left to lose.

He stood there, his fists clenched at his sides, every muscle in his body flexed. He wanted to smash something. He heard a loud, howling scream of anguish, opened his eyes and realized it had been him. Or what had once been him. When the pain peeled away there was only one thought, and it made no sense because it was really a feeling.

Rage.

If Resonance couldn't own the world, he'd destroy it.

He ran the rest of the way back to the north side of the fairgrounds, and headed immediately for the Hollywood exhibit, where he'd worked part-time learning the Fair's layout and schedule.

"Hey, Conrad, you're back," said a young man sitting behind the exhibit's trade table. "Thought you were off for a couple days."

Resonance said nothing. He turned a dial on his wrist and pushed the young man behind a curtain in back of the tent. The curtain shook, then abruptly deflated with a hiss of red mist on the air. Resonance slung the material back into place, barely noticing the blood dripping from inside the tent flap.

The Hollywood Exhibit had an improvised dressing room in back, really just a slop sink and a mirror. He opened a lock-box and fastened a second resonance gun to his wrist. Pulling the tan coat of his summer suit on over it, he glanced in the mirror. Yes, he always looked sharp, he told himself, but he needed something else, a topper. He was Resonance now.

Across the dressing room he saw a forest-green Homburg Stetson hanging in the corner. He tried it on. It fit perfectly. Green, it reminded him of money. The man who had been Conrad Wilcox would have cried, but Resonance smiled and almost laughed as he tilted the hat to one side.

Stepping out of the tent in a slow trudge, he aimed a wrist at The Sky-Ride and then unexpectedly changed his mind. He'd save the Sky Ride for last. Turning southeast, Resonance marched toward the Midway and the crowd with a predatory smile on his face.

Rows of hucksters, barkers, hustlers and pitchmen lined the sawdust lane. All of them yelling, questioning, and joking with the passersby as they tried to entice them into their sideshows and games of chance. Everybody with something to sell, all of them begging for attention from the crowd.

"See the natural Beauties of the Orient! Clad in only what nature gave them!" screamed one barker, purposely ignoring a man exiting the booth who wanted his money back because the girls had worn flowers.

A gyp.

"Be a man of the world! Learn from The Love Machine!" Another gyp.

It was a puppet show.

"Ladies and gents! Ring the bell and win a prize!"

A cheat.

"Three balls for a nickel, son. You don't want your girl to go home with just a kewpie doll, do ya?"

A swindle.

Resonance stepped through the milling crowd, trying to focus his attention only in front of him. He'd passed the Streets of Paris on his way toward the center of the Midway. The barkers back at the more risqué booths had at least been clever, forced to hide the sex in the shows behind the veneer of art and education, but the constant, haranguing repetition from the games vendors began to annoy him.

"Guess your weight and win a prize!"

"Toss a penny on the plate! It's easy!"

"Three rings for a nickel! Just put it over the Coke bottle!"

A cheat, a con, a swindle looking for a dupe, he thought.

Still, Resonance stepped past each diversion seemingly focused on something distant. His stride so unwavering, people in the crowd bumped off of him as he neither noticed nor acknowledged them. As the barker's voices muddled together in an area without much foot traffic, one voice seemed to peel out of the blue.

"Pick a number! Any number! A winner every time!"

Resonance's head suddenly twisted to face the young pitchman standing in front of a vertical numbered wheel. The part-time employee repeated himself thinking he just might close a sale.

"Any number! A winner every time!"

Resonance aimed a wrist at the pitchman. The Midway hawker exploded into a bloody mist as he passed. The people gathering around his bloody clothes hadn't had time to figure out what had happened, and the one man who had witnessed it, didn't believe his eyes. Resonance patted the gun beneath the cloth of his sleeve, glad to be able to use it at maximum force.

The predators grin returned.

Children running to and fro in packs, and the parent's chasing them, little realized they were risking their life as they bumped into the failed executive on the sawdust. Young romantics dared to hold hands across his path. Tourists and mirth makers risked smiling and, worst of all, laughter. All of it wore on the Sonics expert's patience.

But his grin was soon replaced as he rounded the next corner and came to the center of The Midway, where all the action was. There in one plaza stood Ripley's Believe it or Not, and The World of a Million Years ago. The Whirl-O-Plane, and The Living Wonders and Other Freaks of Nature. He stopped and stared at the corner where Ripley's Odditorium and Freak Show shared a spot.

"Freaks and Oddities," the man who had been Conrad Wilcox thought, "Losers. Like me," and turned away. Silently, he trod toward the World of a Million Years Ago. His shoulders sank. He stared at the ground and stopped shuffling his feet.

Standing in the center of the plaza, the man who had been Conrad Wilcox raised his head and turned toward the Whirl-O-Plane ride; two tons of spinning, tilting death, with fifty riders onboard, and a crowd of hundreds around it.

Nobody noticed the man in the homburg fiddling with the cuffs of his shirt. Then he extended his arms.

Chapter 15
THE WHIRL-O-PLANE

"So what happens?" Crankshaft asked, standing outside Mirella's tent.

Mac stared at the ground like he had a problem with it. He stuck his hands in his jacket pocket and fondled his new mask. "Didn't you hear, I'm a knight and a king."

"And?"

"And, we gotta take the fight to them. Chasing around this bastard's loopy clues only seems to get us there after somebody's dead. We need to go back to the Hall of Science; they had tunnels in the walls there. It could be their headquarters."

"Any idea how many guys this 'Resonance' has on his team?"

"Too many. It was like a small army back there, and he managed to bribe Security in case you didn't notice. Damn, I wish we'd driven the Blue Streak!"

Crankshaft didn't ask why. The Bagman's car had a trunk full of guns. The ace mechanic grabbed Mac by the sleeve, and led him toward the loading dock where he'd found the fallen Bagman earlier.

"Remember those security guards we took out," Crankshaft said, out of the side of his mouth. "Before you decided to become one with your bird-brained others?"

"Careful, Crank, I'm King of Knights and all that stuff now."

"Yeah, well I'm your weapons master, or maker, or manager, and you better thank Mirella for that..."

Mac stared impatiently at the mechanic, anxious at both their new-found position, and the time they were wasting circling the Hall of Science instead of going inside.

"...because I put all their hardware in a flour sack and hid it in a box on the loading dock." Crankshaft stepped up on the dock and pointed at a box hidden away in the corner shadows.

"What do we got?" Mac said.

"Seven .45's, six automatics, and one Colt snubnose; all kinds of bullets, and a broken machine gun."

"I'll take the revolver; we'll both carry as many automatics as we can."

"All that hardware, and you still want a revolver?" Crankshaft handed him the pistol.

"No springs to jam up your next bullet." Mac flipped the gun's chamber open and spun it, then grabbed two handfuls of bullets. He stuck the pistol in his shoulder holster, loosening it in the scabbard so it wouldn't stick to the damp leather. "Simple and effective."

"Because you're such a simple and effective guy, huh?" Crankshaft said, not meaning it at all. He popped the clip out of one of the automatics, checked the ammo and racked the slide to make sure it worked. "I checked them all out earlier. Should be OK."

Mac stuffed another automatic in his suit. Crankshaft put the Army Colt under his coat, tucked the bag of pistols into his belt, and headed toward the loading dock door of the Hall of Science.

As Mac reached for the metal door, he heard footsteps on the other side. Slowly, the doorknob began turn. Mac pushed Crankshaft toward the wall behind him and hid behind the door waiting to slam it back into whoever might stick their head around it.

Mac whipped his revolver out of the holster and aimed in front of him. The door opened, then closed to reveal Hunts Helms with a hang dog expression on his face. He looked up from the steps and all he saw was the gun.

"I din't do it! I din't do it!" Hunts jumped back, holding his hands in the air.

Crankshaft stifled a laugh at Mac's irrepressible conman partner-turned-reporter, and the two men stepped out to greet him. Hunts slapped Crankshaft on the back, put his thumbs in his vest, and leaned back smiling.

"Where you been? You're late." Hunts said, as if nothing had happened. "Cops already found the bad guy's tunnels. They're empty; law's got nothing."

"Well, that's what they'd tell you."

"Puhleeeze, Mac. The last thing the cops want is a reporter accusing them of not working a case. They always have 'something developing' at least. I been on 'em like a cheap suit, but alls they got is some kind of cushiony textile from those 'silencers.' Some Australian tourist at the Heidelberg recognized it as a kind of "foamy rubber" they been working on over there."

"He say what they use it for?" Mac said.

"Insulation, stuffing, something to pack things in so they don't bounce around," Hunts answered. "It's new. This guy barely knew about it, but there's a sound researcher at the Sonics exhibit…" he thumbed over his shoulder, "…there where they blow out a candle with sound waves. This Dr. Stoyer just happens to be working on a new way to lessen vibrations in buildings, and he might just be on to something."

"Well great, then we're all thinking, but what do we do?" Mac said.

Without mentioning it, all three men began strolling back to the closed section of the building so they wouldn't be seen. Mac's eyes widened. He snapped his fingers.

"C'mon guys, I've got an idea," he grabbed both men by their suit shoulders and dragged them back toward the loading dock.

Crankshaft and Hunts eyed each other with a look of worry.

"This Resonance character was using the 'foamy rubber' to baffle sound, right? Now who else needs to baffle sound?"

"Radio announcers," Crankshaft said

"Yeah, but the radio station is under full observation." When Mac turned there was a twinkle in his eye. "There's an audience. It's surrounded by windows, and the rear entrance is inches away so the celebrities can get in and out. Who else?"

"Movies," Crankshaft said.

"And what's right by the band shell where the bogus photographer was?"

"Hollywood!" Crankshaft said.

Crankshaft and Mac both started across the fairgrounds again, heading back to where the whole thing had started. Hunts came up from behind.

"Whoa, Mac, hold on. I really think you ought to talk to this Doctor Stoyer guy. He's been working on some kinda'... somethin'."

"But he's still working on it?"

"Yeah, he says there's still some stuff to be done," Hunts said out of the side of his mouth, lighting a cigarette as they walked. "Something about transferring energy somewhere."

"Probably something to do with that 'foamy rubber', huh?" Mac sped up the pace. "I don't know. All this 'science fiction' stuff is out of my league. You want to follow it up?"

"No problem." Hunts stuck his pack of Camels in his vest. "Cops are talking to him, but I don't know who's listening. You guys want to check out 'Hollywood'? I'll play catch up."

Mac nodded. Hunts turned toward the Hall of Science. Mac and Crankshaft ignored the pathway opposite and began crossing the lawn. Halfway to Hollywood, they stopped.

Something high pitched began to wail in an unnatural tone across the lakeshore. The tone lowered. Something exploded, and the earth shook under their feet.

There was a moment when all Mac could hear was the rinky-dink bells and whistles of the Midway then bedlam. It started with shrieking metal, harsh wrenching sounds, clanks and dings, then an explosion and more crashes. Metal against metal, scraping concrete and flying debris. A cloud of smoke appeared over The Midway. Then, screams.

Mac and Crankshaft had taken off at the first squeal. Halfway to Hollywood they were already right by the Midway. First chasing the smoke, then the sound, they ran in the opposite direction of everyone else. After two different people stomped on his toes, Mac started pushing them out of his way. The crowd ran past, some coughing, some crying, as sirens began to wail in the distance. The two were forced to climb off the path, and make their way around the throng fleeing the scene.

"Y'know, Crank, I gotta confess. If we hadn't gotten the pep talk from the Gypsy broad, I'd probably be getting the heck out of Dodge like everybody else."

"Probably be dying from internal bleeding, too. What's the matter, you don't trust her?"

"Crank, I've got a revolver, *and*, an automatic on me; I don't trust anybody."

"Good, because I don't trust you either." Crankshaft lowered his eyebrows, wagged his head and shrugged his shoulders as if to say "so what?"

"Not what I mean, Crank and you know it. The problem is, I start thinking everything I do is..." his eyes rolled up in his head looking for the right word. "...sanctioned...? Yeah, I start thinking everything I do is sanctioned by the gods or the fates or whatever, we both know I'm just going to get into more trouble."

Crankshaft's eyes were wide, then mirthful. He laughed as he pushed his way around a decorative hedge. "You don't trust yourself!"

"Damn right." Mac skated across the damp evening grass rounding both Crankshaft and the hedge to look across the plaza. His jaw hung open. The phrase "It looked like a train wreck" echoed through his head.

People were dead. That was obvious, even without being able to see through the smoke surrounding the wreckage of the Whirl-O-Plane. Shrapnel had been flung hundreds of feet across the plaza, shattering glass, ripping through the pasteboard facades of the temporary buildings, and tearing flesh like a machine age demon.

A scream drowned out the others as a woman clutched her husband's unconscious body in her arms outside Ripley's Odditorium. Blood leaked from the back of his head. The wings of one of the Whirl-O-Planes sat next to him, the scars on the ground where it had bounced leading in a straight line to the small, but ever-expanding pool of blood beneath him.

"You trust Resonance?" Crankshaft said.

Mac said nothing, but trotted over to the wounded man.

The woman with him would have been attractive under any other circumstances. She was young, brunette, with green eyes and long eyelashes. But her voice was wailing and her make up was running. She looked up at Mac for help.

Mac kneeled down beside her and looked at her man's wound. He'd been hit, deep in the belly, just below the rib cage. Right in the liver, Mac guessed. It would be a slow death. The man was lucky he was unconscious.

The woman's pleading eyes met Mac's. He wished he could fix it. She begged for help. He felt helpless.

He propped the man's feet up on some wreckage as one of the Fair's fire trucks thundered on the scene. Some sailors on shore leave were already aiding the wounded. Other men rolled up their sleeves and joined in, moving the rubble to help the wounded and dying. People ran from the doors of building's torn open by the metal shaken from the carnival ride, waving their hands and signaling for help. Mac turned around and saw the torso of a man lying in the street, headless, armless, with just the stump of one leg sticking out.

He stood up and looked away so he wouldn't wretch. His stomach roiled. He gagged involuntarily. Covering his mouth, in the distance he saw a man walking into the entrance of the World of a Million Years Ago exhibit. Strolling! Here the machine age had just exploded all over the beach, and this guy in a homburg, instead of running or trying to help like everybody else, was leisurely sauntering into look at Ripley's Believe it or Not.

Mac didn't believe it.

Sure it was a great chance to sneak inside without paying, nobody was there to take tickets, but it wasn't right. Nobody needed distraction that bad; it was like somebody reading a book on the battlefield. Something about the guy was strange.

And strange was Mac's specialty.

The man in the Homburg turned and stood in the open door, facing the plaza. He looked at Mac. Their eyes met.

The shutterbug! Even without the beard, Mac recognized him. The devious detective's hand ran down his face where he'd just shaved off his own bearded disguise because he'd been working undercover and alarms went off in his head. The shutterbug was his man. And even if he wasn't, he was up to something.

As the smoke cleared from the wreckage, carnies and entertainer's rushed from other exhibits to help the fallen. Freaks from Ripley's Believe it or Not and Mill's Freak show worked beside animal handlers and midgets, digging through the wreckage and providing first aid. Mac saw a young black girl with four legs being carried off by a human skeleton and, for just a moment, wasn't sure whose body parts belonged where. On the other side of the lot he spied Detective Costanovitch and a cluster of policemen. Mac pulled his hat down in front of his face and sashayed in the other direction, toward the Odditorium.

Nobody was there to take his ticket. Mac faced the exhibit's promotional paintings, so Detective Costanovitch wouldn't spot him, and opened the door. The place was dark, other than some of the spotlights on the exhibits, and the occasional shaft of light from the back, probably where dressing rooms were for some of the performers. He could hear something moving there. Making his way toward a spotlight in back, Mac's eyes roamed over the empty exhibits. His quarry was obviously somebody who hadn't come to witness the same wonders as Mr. Ripley.

Something behind all the darkness clattered in the background to his right. More voices could be heard muffled in the thick black and red curtains that enveloped the place.

This was the part Mac hated. He was better at being chased than chasing. Disappearing is easy; you run fast, the more stuff you run by, the more options you have. Chasing, well, you're at their mercy. He thought about how much easier it was to be a crook, and realized he wasn't such a good or bad guy after all. He'd taken the hard road, but he'd taken it to help others. And for the first time, he understood this wasn't just him pretending to have fun, he was helping people nobody else could. Desperate people with no hope, with nothing, just like he had been back when he was a kid.

Mirella might have spotted the paradox. He was using the skills he'd been forced to learn back when he was a dead end kid, criminal skills others hadn't learned because they hadn't seen the world he had; and he'd been given the ability to use those skills against the criminals themselves. What he had yet to realize, what Mirella had neglected to tell him, was that having seen the world from the view underground, he had been given the gift of perspective.

And that perspective had led to a big turn-around for a guy whose only future had been breaking bones for the mob. In the last three months, Mac's motto had changed from "Never give a sucker an even break" to something like "Don't hurt anybody, unless they're asking for it." And now his hands were full.

He stopped thinking about it, and put on the mask. Wedging his hat on over the bag with one hand, he unholstered his revolver with the other and skulked down the dark velvet hallway, listening.

He heard the whine and drone of Resonance's wrist gun, and then a loud crack. A woman's voice, thin and wavering, protested weakly. The sound of a slap peeled in the air, and the sounds turned to weeping.

"Shut up! And get out of here! Out! Out!" the man's voice screeched. "You heard me, you dumb cow! Get up! Get the hell up!"

Another gulped inhalation of desperate air. And then a sob.

Stopping short of the entry, Mac peeked through the heavy velvet curtains surrounding the last exhibit. The room stood lit by one bulb hanging from a wire, shadows did their best to cover the rest of it. It was apparently a maintenance room for the Odditorium. Brooms and mops stood by the door, but clamps, acetylene torches and the smell of chemicals permeated the background. Ripley's had a lot of stage hands, lighting, neon signs, and, it was an all day act. The show never stopped, and the maintenance crew had to be ready for anything. Believe it or not.

A frail, very thin woman lay flat on her back upon a large, comfortable looking cot. But she didn't look very comfortable. Like maybe she was in shock and couldn't move. It sounded like she was trying to speak, but the moaning sounds couldn't be defined as words.

Resonance was backstage half-bent over a tool bench with a hot soldering iron. He tinkered with something on his wrist, then turned and slapped the woman across the face again.

"Get up and get out!" the man in the homburg said, then turned back to the workbench.

Mac could see the solder in one hand and the soldering gun in the other. He was about to jump in and slam Resonance in back of the head, when the Master of Sonics spun and slapped the woman again.

"If you don't move, I'm going to kill you." Resonance backhanded her then came back with another.

Mac saw the sign for the last exhibit in the hall where he was standing and knew why the lady had been taken hostage. The whine and drone of the resonance gun building power filled the air.

Mac backed away, and aimed for an entrance between two of the exhibits so he could slip up behind the man with the sonic cannons. Barely parting the heavy curtains, it was the same scene with a different angle. The man in the homburg hat had his sleeves rolled up. It was the first time Mac had seen the diabolical sonic cannons on his wrist. Resonance was tightening something behind his hand with a tiny screwdriver, grimacing one moment and smiling the next.

"You want to die don't you?" he said, to the prostrate woman raising a hand in the air.

The sound of a .45 revolver's hammer locked and ratcheted behind him.

"Don't flinch," The Bagman said. "Bullets are faster than sound."

Resonance dropped the tiny screwdriver in the sawdust. Mac couldn't see the man's eyes and mouth glare wide with rage, but he did see Resonance clinch his hands.

"Don't." The Bagman's voice was like ice.

"You want to die, too?" Resonance's voice was barely audible.

"After you, snappy." Mac parted the curtains wide, and entered point blank range with his arm straight, gun hand extended. "The lady doesn't doesn't want to die, you dope. Her name's Orpha Ensign, and she's ossified you know, 'The Woman of Stone?' She's got a bone disease. Can't move and her nurse probably ran off. You know you really should case a joint before you just go around shooting off your wrist like that."

Resonance's chest heaved. Mac stood between the woman and Resonance, his gun inches from the back of Sonic terrorist's head. He made eye contact with the woman only a second and saw an acknowledgement of thanks. The strange man with the gun in a sackcloth mask didn't scare her as much her raving abuser.

But all Resonance had to do was bend his wrist.

There was no wailing sound this time, just a high pitch and *Pop!* A table next to the workbench holding chemicals and fuel exploded. One of the curtained walls went up in flame. Mac ducked a blast of fire, but the explosion's concussion hit him a moment later.

All Resonance had to do was finish turning around, his wrist already aimed at The Bagman's chest.

...Mac ducked a blast of fire...

Chapter 16
IT'S CURTAINS!

The Sonic terrorist already had one hand on his wrist as he turned. The Resonance gun whirred, emitted a whooping sound, then cracked.

Mac had a hand to his face, checking to see if his mask was on fire. He cursed through clenched teeth, and let go of his gun as he raised his hands and jumped for the ceiling.

Something grabbed his torso and it started to vibrate.

The ceiling of the Odditorium was covered with the same heavy black velvet as the walls. Mac was almost six-feet; he had earned a living for a while as a burglar, leaping and climbing. His hands and feet clawed at the air above him. His left hand grabbed at one of the seams on the ceiling. His right hand clutched at the other side, trying to tear it open.

The pull of gravity did his job for him. The stitching tore. Falling, he stuck his left hand into slot of fabric he'd opened, and folded the thick fabric in his grip. Then he brought down the house.

The sound of the tearing material drowned out the Resonance gun and the fire. Mac fell to the ground still yanking on the velvet like it was the proverbial rope, trying to cause as much mayhem as he could.

The fabric on the ceiling pulled down the curtains on the walls. The entire backstage collapsed in on itself. At the last possible instant, Mac leapt to his feet beneath the plummeting textile and leaned over the body of the ossified woman, arms spread to protect her from the fallout. Everything went black.

The velvet was thick and heavy. Striking Mac on the back, it knocked the breath out of him, and almost knocked him down on the statue-like woman. Visions of him being the one who crushed her to death held him on his feet, but not upright. Positioning his feet like a weightlifter, Mac bent his knees then lifted from the legs.

Flames still burned only ten feet away from him, the fabric not robbing the fire of the oxygen it needed to grow, but The Bagman didn't know it. Nor did he know Resonance lay face down, temporarily confused but already looking for a way to crawl out of his velvet tomb. He did know he had to move, fast.

"You OK, Miss Ensign?"

"Thank you," she muttered. A tear ran down the side of her face.

Mac heaved one more time, but nothing fell off. He flexed his arms and lowered one to his side. Holding the collapsed ceiling up with his back and shoulders, The Bagman reached into his pocket for his favorite dime store purchase of all time: his Babe Ruth pocket knife.

Even "The Babe" had said it was a good knife.

Mac kept the thing razor sharp. It was small, effective, and once he'd managed to shove the blade through the fabric it worked. Within a minute, he'd cut a slit large enough to pull the ossified woman through.

Mac didn't bother trying to roll her cot out. Instead, he picked the woman up under one arm, and pushed her halfway through the exit he'd carved. Shifting his weight, he swung an arm up so her unmoving form rested on one of his shoulders. With the woman solidly planted on his shoulder, he bent his knees and picked up his hat. Then he stepped outside with the Woman of Stone resting on top of one his shoulder like he was carrying a canoe.

The pasteboard walls in front of the building were still standing and hadn't caught fire yet. Mac trudged down the hallway to the exit, all the while listening to hear if anyone else might be trapped.

Once outside, he put the ossified woman's heels on the ground, and gently lay her on the sawdust outside in the shade of the only bush near the Ripleys Believe it or Not exhibit.

A man in breeches and Willis and Geiger safari gear, probably an animal trainer, dropped what he was doing and rushed over to where Mac was placing a wad of fabric behind the woman's head to use as a pillow.

"Who are you?" the stranger asked, in a stern manner. He had a gun on his hip. He unbuttoned the flap on his holster as he stared at the Masked Man's eyes.

"Mister, I'm the guy that just saved The Woman of Stone. And if you or anybody else around here knows her, I think she could use some comfort right about now."

The trainer continued reaching for his gun. Must've been the burlap mask creeping him out; Mac kind of liked that. His blue-grey eyes stared from the two holes directly into the animal trainer's. The guy was actually going to draw on him.

With Mac kneeling over the disabled woman's body, the animal trainer hadn't even seen him holding his gun beneath the open flap of his jacket. Mac stood up, his revolver aimed right between the man's eyes, while the man still fumbled for his gun.

"This one has real bullets in it," The Bagman said. He knew most animal trainers worked with blanks.

The man stopped fumbling, and held both arms up. "This one would, too. You're just lucky you got the jump on me. I knew something was fishy around here, but I didn't know for sure till the Whirl-O-Plane went up. I saw your partner."

"He is not my partner." Mac's eyes shifted back and forth. There was still so much confusion that most people weren't even looking at them. Then again, it would only take one. He holstered his gun. "You gonna help this lady or aren't you, tough guy?"

The animal trainer gave Mac another stare so wary his head tilted over his epaulets.

"Promise me, you'll help her," Mac said.

"I'll help her."

Mac's back was already to the man walking briskly. "You see that guy in the green homburg, shoot him," he said over his shoulder, and then bounded around the building and back down the long hall of the Odditorium.

The rear right side of the Odditorium smoked more than blazed, in a city made famous by a great fire they'd made sure of that, but the fire was spreading and the smoke debilitating. The one light that had been working had been torn down by the falling velvet ceiling. Mac concentrated on the presence of Resonance so strongly, that for a second he thought about lighting a match, then he remembered the whole back room was on fire.

His mask helped filter the smoke, but he held a hand to his mouth out of instinct. Passing the Woman of Stone exhibit, he rounded the corner into the combination dressing/maintenance room. Other than the smoke, it looked much the same as he had left it. Flames had swallowed the entire rear wall, but were working their way outside faster than inside. Across the room, a few feet away from the wall, sat the roll of heavy fabric that had fallen on top of Resonance.

It was bulging and moving.

The Bagman poked at the pile of fabric with his toe. Something hissed, and fire ate its way through the top of it. Mac stomped on the flame, then on the carpet. Then he started kicking things. Resonance was gone.

Mac pulled off his mask and stuck it in his pocket. His eyes traced the folds in the material on top of everything. He could see one long fold, now burning in the middle that led out between the last two exhibit stages. Almost like a tunnel. Resonance had crawled out.

Back up the hall and out in the Midway, Mac scanned the rescuers and revelers but saw nothing of the sonic terrorist. Watching the crowd he realized how insane the scene was. It was like an explosion had gone off around the Whirl-O-Plane, but everybody in the sea of summer hats a hundred yards away was still having a party. He pushed his hat back on his head and wiped his brow with the back of his hand, searching for Crankshaft. He hated to admit he might need some help.

Across the plaza Detective Costanovitch turned from the crew he'd been talking to and faced Mac's direction. Mac pushed his hat down and melted backwards into the bushes. The less contact he had with the detective the better.

Backing out of the bushes, a hand touched his shoulder from behind. Mac grabbed it and flipped Crankshaft over his shoulder. Crankshaft landed in the bushes.

"Don't do that, Crank!" Mac grabbed the ace mechanic under the arms and helped pull him to his feet, then glanced over his shoulder. Detective Costanovitch was looking directly at him. Mac smiled and waved. The two of them stepped over to one of the metal cars of the Whirl-O-Plane on the ground, lifted it by the wings and pulled it off the path so they wouldn't look suspicious.

Acting like he wasn't trying to get away, Mac remembered his hunch about the Hollywood exhibit. With the Hall of Science sound exhibit shut down where else would Resonance go? As soon as Costanovitch turned around, the two men shuffled off into the darkness between the lights.

"Crank, I think we still need to take a look at Hollywood."

The two men broke into a lope northward for the Hollywood exhibit, still searching for a homburg in a sea of straw hats.

Resonance sat backstage in one of the nomadic "Hoochie Dance" tents littering the out of the way alcoves of the Streets of Paris. He'd only been there twice before, but he had paid the girl for favors of a personal nature; favors that he felt someone like himself shouldn't have to pay for. She gasped when he entered the back of the tent.

"Hey, Sicko! Didn't Leonard tell you to get lost? You get out of here right now or I'll…" She stormed across the floor, one hand winding in the air to slap him.

Resonance pointed a fist at her, and she began to vibrate slowly. One side of his mouth smiled, and he played with the dial on his wrist as she screamed. He liked the way her head exploded first. He'd have to practice that more. Then, as he reached to pull a bathrobe off the wall to throw over the pile of sludge that was the woman's corpse, he saw his face in the mirror.

A whimpering sound escaped his mouth, and he stared at his reflection with dull, glassy eyes. His hand touched his face, and he whimpered again, staring at his hand one moment, then looking in the mirror and sobbing the next.

They had burned him!

Without even bothering to ask him why he did what he did, the man in the burlap mask, that God-forsaken Bagman had set him on fire!

He screamed, loud and long. Resonance had no worry of being discovered. If anything, the scream should have scared people away. Instead, he sat, whimpering, staring at the glass with one of his hands brushing it as if to calm his reflection.

A six inch swath of red crossed his face from the right temple to the left jaw. Bubbles stood out on his flesh and leaked across his face. He could feel his pulse pressing against the raw flesh with every beat. Reflex led him to clamp his hands around his face. The pain forced him to draw them away and as he did, the flesh stuck to his hands. But this time, he did not scream.

He smashed the mirror.

He'd barely escaped with his life, scooting through the wreckage of Ripley's Odditorium on his hand and knees. He had seen the fire in the tunnel before him, but they'd given him no choice. He'd crawled that long mile with the homburg clenched in his hand, laughing at them. And it had burned.

He had thought it would last only a moment, but that one small blaze had been aimed right at him. And nobody cared. The world went on while he suffered. Nobody noticed. They'd written him off.

He clutched a jagged shard from the mirror in one hand, over the dancer's make-up counter. He held it, firmly, until his palm bled. For a furious moment, he dug at one of his wrists with it, but all he could carve were thin shallow lines.

No, he thought, he wouldn't give them the satisfaction of his death.

He stood up, smashed the little desk, and kicked the chair across the tent. He yanked everything off the wall and fell face down on the ground, sobbing. It seemed like a long while passed as he lay there, crying until he could cry no more. He stayed down, sniffling, catching his breath. When he glanced back up he saw the remains of the hoochie dancer.

And he wiped his nose and smiled.

He'd done that.

In this world of evil, he held the ultimate power over life and death. And humanity had failed the test. He'd done what they told him. He had pretended to like, love and care about so much just like he was supposed to. And they had burned him. Him, Conrad Wilcox, no wait, not Wilcox anymore but Resonance. Yes, yes, Resonance! Conrad had been so handsome the hoochie girl had almost stayed with him for free, but even then… No, she'd made him pay. She was like all the rest. A miserable failure and she had needed to be put to death.

Resonance stopped to think, but the thoughts raced through his head with no control. Belief and judgment collided off each other until the worst thoughts of all ricocheted to the top.

His first memory was drowning his younger brother. The spoilt little bastard had never shared his toys. Conrad had been six years old. He'd held the tikes head under the water in a stream behind the house. Dad hadn't been home, and it had taken forever for his little brother to stop kicking and fighting. He pushed the corpse toward the middle of the stream and watched as his brother bounced off logs and over rocks on his way downstream.

Conrad hadn't meant to kill him, but it didn't bother him. If anything, it had made him realize how powerful he was. His mother had known. So he'd arranged her accident, and she had fallen down the stairs in middle of his parent's yearly visit.

Conrad's father might have suspected, but for that reason the deaths were rarely brought up. Conrad remembered his dad, telling him the world was tough and full of people ready to earn their mercenary pay by any means necessary. He remembered the first girl who'd ever loved him and he hadn't felt a thing. He remembered the people he thought were his friends. None was more than an acquaintance and none of them had pretended to like him as much as he had pretended to like them.

He had done what he was supposed to.

He remembered the laughter when he'd blown up the science lab. He could have sworn he'd heard them laughing when the Army had turned him down for the munitions contract. He'd heard their laughter when he went broke. They'd killed his father. They would kill him if they had the chance.

Gritting his teeth, he put his hat on, and realized he was forced to tilt it at a jaunty angle. So manic were his thoughts, a second later he bet himself that if the mirror still worked he'd look like Gary Cooper. He was that far gone.

They had burned him, once. They would kill him if they had the chance. He wouldn't give it to them. They were all going to pay.

Strolling south seemed to have no troubles for him, until he stepped in front of a bright neon display surrounding one of the fountains. A man going the other way spotted the burns on Resonance's face and gasped, his hand covering his mouth. He burst into a fine mist of red as his blood soaked clothes collapsed to the ground.

Resonance could hardly wait for somebody else to look at him like that. Maybe he could do that exploding head thing again.

There was a rumble and a herd of horses ran past. A crowd of thirty people parted around him. Rushing for the exits, they hadn't even looked at him. Two women screamed as a Billy goat chased them around the plaza. More people shuffled by hurriedly, waggling their heads and looking behind them as if to make sure no one was chasing them.

No. They couldn't do that to him! They couldn't leave! Not yet!

He pointed his wrist at the 27th exit to the Illinois Central Station, and watched everything near it shake to pieces. The entrance collapsed. The crowd turned back, twisting, with no idea where to go.

Resonance strolled on. He had to finish this. *They'd turned off the Sky Ride! Damn!* And that was going to be his encore. Oh, well. He decided to make it a brand new intro. Even if it wasn't running, demolishing the highest amusement ride in the world would certainly make an impression. With any luck maybe one of the cars would swing across the fair on its wire and slam into some other expensive novelty. Or even better, maybe a few hundred people.

A young boy in short pants with blonde hair hanging in his face, looked up from the goat he was herding through the crowd just in time to see the Sonic Terrorist. The kid pulled at the neck of his oversized red sweater pointed and shouted to his friends.

"Look, it's the Phantom of the Opera!"

Resonance shoved a fist in the boy's direction. The goat jumped and twisted. The boy chasing it circled behind, and the goat exploded. The six-year old screamed and ducked as he made his way out of the line of fire.

Resonance cursed, his teeth grinding, then suddenly burst into laughter as he pointed the resonance gun at one of the Sky Ride's towers.

Chapter 17
STAMPEDE!

Twelve minutes earlier, halfway to Hollywood, Mac and Crankshaft had stopped dead in their tracks. The film exhibit was surrounded by cops, and the last thing Mac and Crank wanted was for anybody to think they were the villain returned to the scene of the crime. Mac was convinced Mayor Kelly would just love to blame everything on The Bagman, but he only hesitated for a moment.

"Only cop I'm worried about is Costanovitch," Mac said, "and he's still back at the Whirl-O-Plane. I'm going in."

The entire front of the exhibit was crisscrossed with yellow crime scene tape, and three uniform policemen stood in front of the door. Mac pulled his official Tom Mix Ralston Purina radio show sheriff's badge out and looked at it.

"I'm afraid an authentic cop might not think that thing's state issue when they see Tom's name on it," Crankshaft said.

"Maybe if I rode up on horse." Mac put the badge back in his pocket.

They circled the tent until they heard voices in back. A nasal voice asking questions and a very clear voice answering them. Maybe one of the actors. They stood there a moment trying to listen through the rear exit, but the noise of the scattering crowd and the sound-baffled walls left them both shrugging their shoulders. They couldn't make out the words.

"Damnit. I shouldn't have let Hunts go after that scientist," Mac said. "He could just walk in and tell us everything we need to know. I can smell this Resonance guy here, Crank. I think I need to wait and ask some questions."

Crankshaft shrugged his shoulders again.

"Hey, Crank, can you do me favor?"

"Oh, hell no! I'm the armorer, remember? You're the designated hero. Me, I want my cut."

"You want to stop Resonance?"

"Of course."

"Tonight that's your cut."

Despite his arguments, Mac knew that Crankshaft's complaints were more about warning The Bagman from danger than trying to avoid it. The ace mechanic would do almost anything for Mac, and had proven it on more than one occasion.

After a short explanation, Crankshaft went off to retrieve the top of the Gypsy fortune teller's empty tent. The broad piece of cloth that hung over the open top for ventilation, when removed would be a piece of fabric some twelve feet square with a rope already attached to all four corners.

While the police continued to question people in back of Hollywood, Mac went around front to ask the police officers on duty what happened. They said only that there had been an emergency and the exhibit was closed for the day. Mac waved a hand in the air.

"Look around lately? You might think about closing the whole fair."

The cop gave him the eye, said "Just between you and me..." and told Mac about the murder.

After he mentioned the Mayor's Medal ceremony, there was no doubt it was Resonance.

Mac scanned the skyline, wondering if the killer might have given up. At least some of the people were leaving the fairground. The Sky Ride had been closed, which was a relief not only because Resonance could aim from it at anywhere in the park, but also because Mac had almost been killed by the thing and never wanted to see it again.

A few minutes later, a young, blonde haired man stepped out of the Hollywood exhibit. Mac said he was sorry to bother him, waved his Tom Mix badge in the air as fast as he could and started asking questions.

The young man introduced himself, and told Mac to call him "Walter." He explained that while he hadn't worked at the Hollywood exhibit, he'd been hanging around there all day considering a career in broadcasting. He explained that while a crew of Hollywood professionals was on duty most of the day, the actual exhibit employees numbered only four. One was dead, two were at home taking the day off, and the other had disappeared. His name was Conrad Wilcox.

"Can you tell me anything about him?"

"Wilcox...Conrad Wilcox," the young man said, closing his eyes to concentrate. He tapped his forehead with the side of his fist, and began to speak in rote like he was reading the information off the back of a card. "Son of millionaire industrialist Randolph Wilcox. His dad committed suicide a few years back after trying to expand his investments right before the crash. Attended...? Yale, I think...has a reputation for being a cold fish. Plays the horses and played polo in college, but he got kicked out after he blew up a science lab. Then he founded his own company... Radio dynamics? Radio Enterprises? Something like that."

"Any idea what they do?"

"Did," Walter answered. "They declared bankruptcy a few months back. Rumor had it he was working on some kind of electrical musical instrument, but Joseph Theremin and Ondes Martenot beat him to it."

"So he's some kinda' F. Scott Fitzgerald, Jazz Age electrician?"

"Sounds like it, doesn't it? But there was something in the financial pages about him losing a weapons contract with the army. Seems like they said he needed more research. Whatever it was, the government shut him down."

"Weapons contract, huh." Mac clamped his fist around his jaw and massaged it a second. "This Wilcox, he lose a bundle in the market, too?"

"Rumor has it. Mark, one of the exhibit hosts, said Wilcox had once been fixed for life. Said he was a quiet guy too, always tinkering, never even had lunch with anybody."

"Think he's got a chip on his shoulder?"

"Five years ago he had millions, now he's working part-time at the fair." Walter's head snapped up, and his eye's widened. "Hey, besides the Hollywood murder, you think he might have something to do with all the other stuff going on around here tonight?"

"I don't know, but you might want to think about taking cover yourself. Something smells rotten in Chicago."

"I think that's the stock yards, mister." Walter smiled because Mac had. "Besides, I'd kind of like to find out what's going on."

"Well, be careful, OK? And thanks." Mac slapped the young man on the back. A few yards away he turned and yelled, "Hey, Cronkite! You'd make a hell of a newsman."

The young man's eyes shifted sideways as he mulled over the thought, watching Mac's back as the Criminal Crime Fighter cut through the thinning wave of fairgoers.

Mac circled around Hollywood one more time, anxiously awaiting Crankshaft's return. Eyeing the band shell where the foreign dignitaries had been murdered only a few hours before, Mac actually felt a chill in the summer evening. He could still feel the presence of Resonance in the park, almost as if someone was watching him.

A rolling stone may gather no moss, but it also makes a lousy target, Mac told himself. He had to keep moving. He could come back and get Crankshaft later. Now where would he go if he needed to hideout at the Fair? Mac could think of only one place. The Streets of Paris.

He stopped before he'd taken a step. Mac had never been a hero, so he wasn't too sure what a hero would do. Sure, he wanted to go to The Streets of Paris, but that was him. Being crowned the King of Thieves just added a strange responsibility to the problem, while being the Knight of Cups meant he would either accomplish great things, or be destroyed by them. It was that last part that bothered him. And even if he could pull off this great thing, whatever it was, would it matter? He glanced at his watch, thinking he had to make better use of his time. What would a hero do?

What would Sam Spade do? Probably go to the Streets of Paris.

The Shadow? No fair, he already knows everything.

But Tarzan, Tarzan would get a rope. So would the Lone Ranger and

Kid Wolf. He didn't think about the fact that the last two were cowboys, just that they were heroes and if they could use a rope, so could he.

Mac turned left before he reached the Streets of Paris, then steered east toward the Agriculture and Livestock exhibits. The further he headed lakeside toward the back of the fair, the more people he saw. As far as he knew Resonance was still alive, and they were all in danger. After he got a rope, he'd find a way to run the crowd off.

Might even be fun.

Passing an unmanned information desk, Mac picked up a clip board and a pen, and kept walking east as if they belonged to him. The first of the gated livestock were goats, and while Mac had heard of a goat roper, he'd never seen one, and thought he'd be more likely to find a rope with the cattle and horses. About halfway past the hundredth stall containing either a sheep or a chicken, he spotted a prize winning bull sporting a blue ribbon. About fifty yards behind the bull was a corral with about a dozen horses penned in it. At the back of the corral sat a barn with a hayloft.

Mac pulled the bolt on the gate and let himself in, skirting the edge of the corral. Having half grown up on the road, Mac had dealt with his share of horses, most of them having tried to scrape him off on some barbed wire. Luckily, the horses made room for him, and he strolled around the edge of the corral clipboard in hand, trying to look like a cowboy by walking as bow-legged as he could. A gent wearing a red shirt and a yellow bandana pushed the barn door open and stopped him.

"Only official livestock exhibitors are allowed past this point, mister."

Mac held up his clipboard, quickly waved his fake badge and stuck it back in his pocket. "Muh name's Goodnight, I'm one of the judges. Just checkin' the barn for inventory. Would you mind answering a few survey questions?" Mac's experience had taught him that nobody expects a criminal to hang around asking questions.

"Survey?" The cowboy spit, and then smiled. "Well sure." The cowhand led Mac next to the barn door.

Mac's survey consisted of asking the man how many animals and what kind were at the exhibit. Did he think the fair had given equal opportunities for each animal to be judged, and did he think there was an easier way to manage feed and care for the animals. The whole affair took all of three minutes. Mac thanked the cowboy, and the grinning cowhand moseyed off toward the Agricultural Building.

Without so much as looking around, Mac stepped into the barn. Three waxed rodeo ropes hung right by the door. Grabbing one of the coils and slinging it over his shoulder, Mac picked up a bucket and headed back out of the corral. The big man with the bucket almost looked as if he belonged there.

Twice he almost hit somebody with the metal pail and realized he needed to find a way to get the crowd out of harms way.

As he reached the gated Livestock pens nearer the entrance, providence smiled at him. About halfway down the lot, five, scrappy-looking, under-aged denizens of the deep city huddled around a pen, taunting a goat. One of them trying to feed it while another seemed to be trying to sneak up behind it and tie a string of tin cans to its tail. It was the same gang of kids he'd bribed to find out who was guarding the gates. His dead end kids.

"Did you guys use the money I paid you to get in the Fair?"

The ten-year-old wearing a baseball cap eyed the six-year-old in the baggy sweater. It was obvious to Mac, the younger child was supposed to have been their look out, and had messed up by letting an adult get near them.

"In all honesty, sir, we did," said the youngest boy, his bangs falling in his face."

Mac dropped the bucket, put a hand over his heart, and began speaking like a ham actor mimicking the kid. "'In all honesty, sir' most people who start a sentence with that phrase are lying, kid."

The boys looked at each other, then looked up at Mac staring them down.

"Honestly, mister…" The oldest boy spoke, and caught himself before Mac's evil eye drilled another hole in him. "OK, OK, we snuck in. There's a board in the back fence we loosened, been using it to sneak in since the fair opened."

"Good," Mac said. "I'd hate for you boys to pay and then have to leave. That money I gave you's for food and shelter."

"Some old Gypsy lady was guardin' the fence earlier and we couldn't get in," the youngest said, pawing at the cuff of his short pants.

Mac's brow furrowed. Had Mirella set up his entire earlier meeting with these little wiseguys? "A Gypsy, huh? So she left and then you guys came around back?"

"She almost waved and told us to come on in," the boy in short pants said.

One of Mac's eyebrows lowered in thought, as he momentarily pondered Mirella's possible plan. Then he knew why.

"Would you guys like to make a little extra money?"

Five young hands raced up, waving in the air.

"Y'know all the explosions and stuff that have been going on?"

"Happens every day, Mister," the youngest said cynically.

"The Whirl-O-Plane blows up everyday?"

The oldest boy stepped forward, pushing the youngest back. It was obvious he didn't want the little scrapper to talk them out of a job. "No… No, it doesn't happen everyday. Jackie's just talking about the fireworks."

"Well, there's going to be a lot more than fireworks going off, guys. It's going to get dangerous. But you should be able to watch the whole show from across the street on Michigan Avenue." Mac pulled out his wallet. "Here's the deal. I give you each two dollars now, and then, you go by this cigar store…" Mac handed them a card for his cigar store. "…and I'll pay you another buck."

The boys were already extending their hands without even asking what the job was.

"You want us to beat somebody up?" the pint-sized Jackie said, pounding one fist into another.

"No," Mac said. "Nobody gets hurt. This one requires stealth."

"Stealth?" the kid in knickers and a flat cap said.

"Nobody can even know you're there," Mac said, "like thieves in the night."

"Mister," the oldest boy said, "we were never here."

"Perfect," Mac said. "See, I'm trying to get people out of the park so they won't get hurt, and I need you to help get them out of here."

"Ya want us to scare 'em off?" Pint-size held a fist up.

"Not like that, Jackie. What I need you to do is…" Mac held a hand to his mouth and spoke quietly, "…open every single pen in the livestock area, and let the animals out."

"Stampede!" the pint-sized kid cheered, his fists bouncing at his sides.

An evil but joyful smile crossed the face of the two older boys. The oldest one pulled two dollars out of the fan of bills in Mac's right hand, and a card out of his left. The rest of the boys lined up behind him.

Mac turned and hurried through the crowd, pulling the lariat back up on his shoulder. With most of the animals in separate stalls, the odds of a stampede were against the boys. Still, he knew they'd raise some hell.

Three minutes later, a dozen horses came galloping down the path, as passersby leapt for the grass, some even climbing trees. As the thundering hooves passed them by, Mac couldn't help but yell along with the kids, "Stampede!"

After the livestock had passed, though, he felt the ground still shaking. He heard what sounded like the pint-sized kid screaming about "the Phantom of the Opera." And then, the now familiar winding sound, two separate high pitched tones cutting through the air, and then merging into one. Something exploded, and more screams erupted from the milling crowd.

Mac heard something *crack* above the lagoon, almost like metal buckling. He glanced up just in time to see two cars from the Sky Ride plummeting down their support wires. Six tons of metal aimed directly at the crowd gathered on the Midway.

Chapter 18
THE SKY FALLS

From a distance, The Sky Ride looked like two toothpick towers with a string running between them but up close it was gigantic. Four elevators ran on each tower, twenty-three stories high. Ten Rocket Cars, trailing steam just like the spaceships in a Flash Gordon serial, held thirty-six passengers and weighed in at 6200 pounds each. Counter balances weighing almost as much as the cars sat some hundred feet apart on the wires. The entire thing cost the combined efforts of five corporations and about 1.4 million dollars to erect.

Mac watched as a million dollars worth of it fell down. There was the sound of the engine winding and then droning as the tones of the Resonance Gun matched those of the rides lift wires. Then, the wrenching sound gave way to a snapping metallic clang. The cables holding the cars in the air snapped.

The south tower catapulted northward, then back, and the air filled with a *zinging* sound as the lift cable whiplashed from the rocket car's runners and across the lagoon.

Mac watched as everything seemed to move like a car wreck, in slow motion. South, on the far side of the lagoon, two of the rocket cars plummeted straight to the earth. One rolled in the air, bounced off the bridge beneath, and spun into the lagoon. The second car plunged straight down, collided with the edge of the observation deck, then rolled through the glass storefront of the Walgreen's exhibit.

The shore closest to Mac stopped one spinning car from colliding with the crowd on the plaza. But, with the first car blocking his view, Mac couldn't see the one behind it, swinging like a pendulum through the air right at him.

A chill ran from the back of Mac's neck to the front of his scalp. Then, suddenly, a high pitched sound cut the atmosphere, drowning out even the crashes and screams of the whirling wreckage.

"Get down!" Mac screamed without thinking as he hit the dirt. The thick iron cable snapped, ricocheted off the north side of the lagoon and whiplashed into the crowd on the plaza. Mac's head popped up just in time to see the second rocket car ski over the water and hit the grass. The car bounced and rolled.

Mac sprinted and jumped.

Pitching himself sideways, the big man body-blocked a dozen fairgoers still frozen with shock, pitching them down and out as the rocket car dug into the earth inches away. Mac slammed on top of a small family, grinding them in the dirt as the car careened off the ground. He turned over just in time to see the six-thousand pound behemoth flipping in the air above him. A prayer raced through his head as it hung there. Finally, after what seemed a hushed eternity, the car hit the ground on the other side of the crowd.

When it hit, Mac realized he was lying on the ground with his feet pulled up over his head. Without a thought he rolled, and came up on his feet, pushing through the crowd, southbound.

But the crowd was headed north. Panicking.

It had been easy for people to miss Resonance's evil plot when he'd been building to his crescendo. It was simple to miss one, tiny, carnival attraction breaking, or a single murder taking place unseen acres away. But this was the Sky Ride, the biggest, tallest, most expensive ride ever built, the ride that made all the headlines. And nobody wanted to make it into the obituaries.

Those that didn't clamor for the nearest gates made for the beach, even the fair employees. Panic caused more panic. The crowd around the 31st street gate bottlenecked as the onrushing swarm began to push and trample people under their feet. Uniformed police blew whistles to no avail, as the crowd screamed over shrill warnings and ignored their waving arms.

Mac didn't have to look. He knew what was going on. He could feel it. They'd been cornered like an animal with everything to lose, and the only thing worse than a man with nothing to lose, was a crowd of them. Something blared out of one of the loudspeakers mounted on poles throughout the park. A cop fired a gun in the air, and some of the people stopped.

Not Mac. With his background, bedlam was practically a scientific method. He lowered his head and shoved his way south. Rounding the lagoon he saw the smart-mouthed little blonde-haired kid running in circles and several people laying on the ground. At least three piles of blackish-pink clothing stuffed with human gore sat scattered near them.

Mac's head pivoted like a bird's. A green homburg stood out in the distance heading southeast. The Man of Steal hit the pavement, shoving people out of his way, pinballing through the crowd and hopping over hedges. He bounced off the chest of a man six inches taller and a hundred pounds heavier.

"Think you're tough, don't you, bully?" the man said, shoving Mac backward with both hands. He could have been the side show's strong man.

"Sorry, buddy, I just…"

The strong man shoved at him twice more, looking for a fight.

Mac pulled out his gun and shot him in the foot.

...the six thousand pound behemoth flipping...over him.

The crowd parted. Mac was on his way with his hat pulled over his face before they'd even spotted the strong man. The green hat kept moving in the opposite direction. So did his pursuer.

A woman ran by Mac and broke into a scream so loud he almost fell in the opposite direction. When he looked back up he couldn't find the green hat amidst the all the straw ones. He twisted and turned in the swarming throng, cursing, before he remembered to put his gun back in the holster. Climbing up on a park bench to look, he thought he might have just seen an emerald hat headed around the corner of The Temple of Mystery.

He was cutting through the throng of curiosity seekers rushing out of the two-headed baby exhibit, when he noticed a man in a blue uniform on top of the Temple of Mystery, wielding a high powered rifle and perched behind the gigantic head of an Egyptian pharaoh. Glancing up to his right Mac saw another one perched across the street.

"Oh great! Sniper cops. Might as well just jump off another airship…" Mac slapped himself in the head, and began muttering a list of horrible deaths as he forced his way through the panicking crowd. "…no, I'll stand in front of the Shooting Gallery, maybe wrestle an alligator…"

He was considering suicide by Kraft Kitchen Mayonnaise when he realized the crowd was thinning out. Crankshaft stood across the lot with the top of Mirella's tent bundled under his arm.

"I thought you were going to wait for me in Hollywood."

Mac put a hand on his partner's shoulder as he tried to pass by, almost ignoring him. "No time, Crank! Bad guy that way." He pointed.

Crankshaft turned and walked with him. Mac stopped and pivoted his head some more.

"Damnit! No! I lost him." He rushed to corner of the nearest back alley, looking back and forth in all four directions. "He's wearing a green homburg, like Capone's, y'know?"

"Capone's was black." Crankshaft tossed the bundle of tent cloth at Mac.

Mac glanced up at the last second, and managed to catch it. "But it was a homburg."

"Maybe we should go to the Bavarian exhibit."

"Yeah, or Homburg." Mac pulled out a cigarette and lit it, pushed his hand under his hat and ran his fingers over head. "I don't like this guy, Crank. He's crazy."

Crankshaft's eyebrows lowered. One side of his mouth smiled at the irony.

"He needs power," Crankshaft said.

"He's got power," Mac said, smoke coming out of his nose.

"He needs more, probably electrical power. Whatever those sonic guns shoot are going to eat up a lot of it."

"Like that Big Bertha diesel generator?" Mac thumbed over his shoulder in the direction of the exhibit.

"Yeah, but he's going to need to move around; that thing weighs five tons."

Mac turned in circles looking like a kid trying to make himself dizzy and then stopped and snapped his fingers. "Look up."

"Why, you going to untie my shoelace?"

"No, Crank, I'm not." He spoke the words slowly, seriously. Not like himself. "Look up. You'll see snipers."

"Bullets do travel faster than sound." Crankshaft tugged on Mac's arm trying to get him moving again, didn't matter where. He knew Mac thought best when he was moving.

"Yeah, but what if he's doing the same thing."

Crankshaft's jaw fell open. "Running for high ground like the snipers..."

A tiny, high pitched sound emitted in the background. Then it began increasing in volume. Two tones warbling two dangerous notes danced in the air, lowered, and then raised in pitch like a radio trying to receive a weak signal. The squealing danced on the periphery of ultra high frequency.

Something short-circuited then roared electronic feedback. The sound cracked and exploded over their heads, and pieces of the sniper rained down on the other side of the street.

Mac couldn't see him, but he heard Resonance laughing. The Bagman glanced in the other direction and saw nothing but a police uniform hanging over the edge of the parapet. It was dripping blood and the blue uniform looked purple.

Crankshaft charged right for the "Western Saloon" across the street; Mac ducked into the building on his left, The Temple of Mystery!

A ticket taker stood inside the door ignoring the evacuation outside. Mac spread his hand over the man's face and pushed him out of the way, James Cagney style. Running toward the theater's stage, he stopped in the aisle for an instant, and then turned around.

The heavy whirring sound was getting louder, but coming from in front of the building. Trotting, Mac raised his arm as he approached the ticket taker. The ticket taker backed away. Mac unholstered his .45 and peeked between the two swinging doors at the entrance. Resonance was floating down the middle of the street.

The sonic terrorist wore some kind of backpack battery now. A series of white surges circled him in the air, surrounding him like heat waves coming off concrete in the summertime. The circular globe of energy floated down the avenue, with Resonance walking in the center it. Mac couldn't even see his feet touch the ground, but the ball kept rolling up the street.

He stood at the door's edge watching, waiting for a shot. Across the street, a uniformed policeman came into view atop the game emporium.

Aiming a high-powered rifle at the man in the force field, the officer got two shots off. Nothing happened until, almost as an afterthought, Resonance turned, waving his wrist at the man. Mac watched the policeman pop and melt like all the others.

A giant sphere of pulsing, sonic energy made its way down the center of the street with Resonance standing in the middle of it. The orb of sound seemed to bend the light, its exterior reflecting colors in different wavelengths like oil on top of a stream, all the while pulsing with a vibrating roar so deep and perhaps out of the range of human hearing that the ground shook beneath Mac's feet.

He felt like a mouse peeking out of its hole as the big ball of power rolled right by him on the other side of the wall. He knew bullets wouldn't take it out, at least not so far. He looked up through the crack in the door just in time to see Crankshaft across the street.

Mac stood behind the sonic sphere waving his arms and waggling his head "No!" Resonance passed and couldn't see him. Crankshaft ducked out of sight behind the parapet, then reappeared with a bucket in his hands. Mac continued to signal *no*, waving his hands and head frantically. With Resonance directly beneath him, Crankshaft dumped two gallons straight down.

The water poured off the sound. Again, waves of color like the film on a soap bubble formed in the air, glistening. The sonic sphere was a wall of solid sound.

Resonance looked up at the Western Saloon building, but saw nothing. He had hardly noticed. Grim resolution set sternly on his face, his eyes narrowed. Focused only on the space in front of him, Resonance rolled down the Midway.

He hadn't even noticed them.

People weren't getting blown up anymore, though. The men with guns had learned better and were hiding. There were still people in the park, but most were walking for the exits or at least headed off the Midway. The sane and smart ones.

Mac and Crankshaft, however, were standing in the middle of the street.

"What the hell was that?" Mac's mouth still hung partially open

"A job for the coast guard, most likely," Crankshaft said. "I thought I might be able to electrocute him, but what he's got now is a whole new kind of weapon." Crankshaft said. "Where is he getting all that power?"

"I was thinking he might have a battery in that backpack he put on."

"He's pushing more than two thousand amps. I don't see how it would fit."

"Radio Power?"

"You think he'd want money if he could broadcast power over a radio?" Crankshaft said.

Before Mac could shrug his shoulders, the drone and whirr of Resonance and his sonic force field began to fade but not in the distance. Mac had expected to hear the energy field buzz off into the distance, but what he heard was more like a gap in the sound. Like somebody had just turned the volume knob down. *Maybe this guy didn't have that much power.*

Out of the blue, the buzzing faded to a hum, then a whirr. Moment by moment, the dynamo's roar seemed less than it had the second before. It faded, then all but shut down.

Mac and Crankshaft glanced at each other and took off running in the direction of the fading, sporadic drones and buzzes. Resonance rounded the corner of the Irish village. The King of Thieves and his buddy stopped with their back to the wall, then slid around the corner. But Resonance was gone.

Guns drawn, the two men scuttled up the street, shifting positions and aiming all around them as they made their way to the next intersection.

When they got there they stopped. Both men stepped into the center of the street. Resonance was nowhere in sight, nothing but a feeling left in the air. A strange sort of vacancy. Despite the screaming passersby, despite the hustle of emergency workers and small packs of roving curiosity seekers, despite even the ringing in Mac's ears, a silence seemed to hang in the air. But the smell of death hung on a trail of burnt ions that floated across the plaza like smoke.

They turned right and glided back toward the Midway. Mac knew where Resonance was headed. He'd known all along.

Straight back down The Midway the two men strode. Mac loosened his revolver in the holster. Crankshaft checked his .45, racked the slide and put a bullet in the chamber. When they hit the plaza, they took a path behind some small booths, so as to have cover from whatever stood to the east. They stopped at the nearest corner, backs to the wall.

"You see him?" Crankshaft said.

"No, but he's here. I can smell him. This is it for him. The big show. The tallest thing left standing? The Cyclone. See, the Big Bertha generator may have more power, but from there you can't see anything. Our boy, Res', he not only has to see what's coming, but he wants to see everything he can destroy."

"Sounds like you think you've figured this guy out."

"Aw, he's angry at the world like every other would-be genius in prison. Except in his mind it's perfectly acceptable to kill people…" Mac snapped his fingers "…like that! Without a thought! People are bad enough just pointing guns around and shooting, but this guy's killing people without thinking about it. By the time he's killed one, he's already looking forward to the next. Anybody that can think like this guy is sick beyond belief."

"But *you* know he's going to be across the street at the rollercoaster." Crankshaft deadpanned.

"I have a gift, Crank. Without it, all I could depend on is your bubbly effervescent attitude." Mac pulled his new mask on and shrugged his shoulders.

Crankshaft noticed Mac's comment sounded funny, 'ha-ha,' until the mask covered the big man's eyes. Then it was funny, 'weird.' Mac was The Bagman now. You couldn't figure him out either.

"Besides, I do know this guy," Mac's voice was like ice. "I used to be like him."

Crankshaft felt a chill fill the vacancy that had hung over the Midway. The Bagman wedged his hat on over his mask and peeked around the corner. Slowly his eyes went wide, reflecting the light from across the lot.

"Wow. This guy's insane, Crank."

Chapter 19
GUTS ON THE TRACKS

Mac stepped out into the street as if he belonged there, walking with a powerful stride. Crankshaft met him with his gun in his hand. Neither moved for a moment, then, without acknowledging each other, they both advanced into the shadows beneath an awning, next to the world's largest rollercoaster.

The man who had been Conrad Wilcox now stood at the highest point of the awesome Cyclone's track. Behind him, two cables ran directly from the track and up the back of his shirt, as if he'd plugged himself into the third rail. In front of him, beneath sleeves rolled up in wads above his elbows, two leather straps held sonic blow torches on his wrist. He was already glowing inside the pulsing orb formed from the mere readying of the resonance guns. He almost danced, his body swooning like a ham actor's in a Broadway melodrama, his arms following the directions he pretended to fall. There was a contented smile on his face, but his eyes reflected only the blackness of the dead air around him.

Beneath the awning where crowds normally stood in line for hours to get to the rollercoaster, the two heroes loped over and around the ticket gate. A series of steps led up to a boardwalk where the crowd would wait in short sections to board their rollercoaster car. To reach the coaster's track on the opposite side, to even look get a look at Resonance, you had to stand out in the open.

Don't stand out in the open, Mac thought.

He turned left, looking almost as if he had been headed in that direction all along. Beneath the faux concrete ceiling, stood a carnival worker in white coveralls with carpenters pockets and loops sewn into the hips. The coaster mechanic held his hands in the air with his eyes closed, yelling.

"I didn't see nothing. I didn't see nothing. I didn't see nothing..." he repeated.

"Well, what good are you then?" The voice spoke quickly, every consonant sharp, every vowel cutting. Echoing off the walls like something solid. "Seriously, help me or I'll shoot you."

The ranting mechanic was speechless. His mouth opened, but no sound came out.

Crankshaft started to cross the walkway to talk to him. The mechanic almost sighed. Mac waved the gun and everybody else jumped back.

"Where's the generator?" The Bagman said.

"Over there." The mechanic lowered his hands, wiped one on his pants leg, and pointed toward the open space in the middle of the Cyclone. A hundred yards away on the other side of the rollercoaster sat a generator the size of a tour bus.

"Shut it down!" The Bagman yelled.

"Can't do it," the mechanic yelled, and pointed through the ceiling, where Resonance stood overhead. "He said he'd kill anybody going near the thing."

Mac sized up the situation, then his head collapsed backward between his shoulders. The generator was out in the open, under dozens of strings of Christmas lights so everybody could see it. But there was definitely no cover there, and he had seen Resonance looking in the same place earlier. He was keeping lookout from the crow's-nest.

Mac couldn't even tell if the big diesel generator was running or a back up. He leaned into a band of light behind him, and his shadow appeared some twenty feet across the concrete lot where the engine was parked. He heard two different tones hum and whirr in the air in front of him as shimmering reds and yellows glistened in a sheet of wind near the opposite fence. He stepped back in the shadows and a wave of light and sound disappeared.

"We can knock it out, but it wouldn't do us any good, anyway," Crankshaft said. "The coaster was wired into the same system as the Planetarium. The power's locked on for the entire fair."

They could hear the pulsing hum above them growing louder. Mac pitched to the left crossing to where the mechanic stood frozen. Crankshaft followed as The Bagman climbed up the down staircase ordinarily used by customers exiting the rollercoaster. Even with the rest of the noise, he could feel the power humming from the Cyclone's tracks. Gazing between the pine floorboards of the boardwalk above, he could see Resonance ensconced in a swirling circle of light and sound, his smile wide, his eyes dead.

A man in World's Fair Security uniform holding a .30-06 rifle found his way through the chain link fence, and made a break for the generator. The whine grew higher and the hum grew lower, milky fibers appeared in the air around him like webs in a puddle. Halfway across the lot the man in uniform's eyes went blank. He looked unconscious, but his feet kept moving. Mac could see blood pouring out of the man's ears as the security guard pitched forward face down on the concrete.

"How're we going to stop this guy, Crank. Every time we get a look at him he almost kills us. I mean, we show ourselves, he shoots and runs, and the whole thing starts all over again. We have to end this thing here."

Mac suddenly realized he could feel the power running through the Cyclone's tracks but the ride wasn't moving.

"How come the coaster cars aren't running?" he yelled at the mechanic.

"There's a switch between the two tracks, like a railroad switch." The carnie pointed through the exit hole cut in the floorboard above him, toward the track and two rows of cars sitting next to it. "Press the handle and pull, the cars file out on the line. Right before he killed the ticket taker, that guy threatened to kill anybody on the inside of the Cyclone's fence. You go out there you'll die like everybody else!"

Mac's hands ran over the top of Mirella's tent packed under his arm as if the fabric might give him the answer. It didn't. Crankshaft sidled up next to him.

"We can distract him, or try to use camouflage."

"Camouflage it is," Mac said. "He seems to be killing anything that gets his attention."

Crankshaft stepped back into the shadows where he'd seen a wooden shipping pallet leaning against the fence, and stepped back out a second later holding it over his head. "The wood will almost match the boards on the waiting platform. You may have to make like a sloth, though. Move too fast and he'll spot you."

"Move too slow and I make a great target. Either way my guts end up all over the tracks." The Bagman grabbed the pallet out of Crankshaft's hands and hoisted it over his head. "Here goes nothing."

"Yo, Mac!" Somebody yelled from behind the turnstile. "...I mean, Yo! Bagman! Mister *The* Bagman!" Hunts Helms, Mac's old buddy, yelled doing his sarcastic best to keep Mac's secret identity a secret.

Hunts was carrying a metal bucket with one hand and pulling a short, stout man in a white lab coat with the other. He stopped in front of Mac and slung the man in the lab coat before the masked man.

"Mister Bagman, sir, this is Doctor Leonard Stoyer. I tried to talk to you about him earlier. He's one of General Electric's sound experts. The guy with the invention that "baffles sound!"

"Foam rubber?" Mac and Crankshaft said in unison.

"Not foam rubber!" the tiny doctor said, putting the two buckets he'd been carrying on the ground. "Paint."

Something in the courtyard beyond them cracked. Somebody screamed their last breath.

"Paint..." Mac said, standing with his fingers open like victory had just slipped between them. "You're going to stop this madman...with paint."

"Not just any paint, Mr. Bagman," the doctor said, "Vipraintium!"

"Vipraintium?" Crankshaft didn't like the marketing. "Because it's 'praint'?"

Doctor Stoyer grabbed Crankshaft by the lapels. "It's paint that absorbs vibration!"

"'Vibrapaint' or maybe 'Absorbacoat'? Something like that would sound better." Crankshaft swiped the tiny doctor's hands from his jacket.

"Shut up. Both of you." The Bagman's voice silenced them with almost a whisper. "You can call it whatever you want. What's it do?"

"Vipraintium was designed to lessen sound vibrations in standing structures, whether the sounds are of the musical studio variety or the excess noises of the city." Dr. Stoyer spoke like it was part of a presentation he'd already given a hundred times. "It converts sound waves to heat."

Mac and Crank both did a double take.

"How hot?" Mac asked.

"Well, see that's the problem..." Dr. Stoyer began.

Mac slapped his hand over the doctor's mouth. "I think we've got enough problems at this point, Doc. Let's say Resonance hits me with two tones that vibrate me to death, how long before I pop?"

"Well, we're still perfecting the exact parameters for 'vipraintium...'" the doctor began.

"It gets really hot, Mac...er, Bagman." Hunts Helms shoved Dr. Stoyer out of the way. "Then it bursts into flame."

"So instead of vibrating to death, I burst into flame. Great plan there, Hunts."

"Whatever you paint will get hot, vibrate and then burst into flame. It'll buy you time. Maybe help whatever plan you have."

"So far the plan seems to be painting myself and then bursting into flame," Mac said. "We can't beat this guy toe-to-toe. We've got to play him. Suck him in. Doc, if I pour a bucket of that paint over my head, get hit with earthquake, hurricane, and sonic storm vibrations, how long till I turn into a Roman candle?"

"Vipraintium is still in the experimental stage, I'm afraid. Mr. Helms has made it about as clear as I can." The doctor took off his glasses and polished a lens with his handkerchief. "It gets hot. As soon as whatever has been painted begins to vibrate, you have anywhere from five seconds. Then..." he rubbed two fingers together. "Poof!"

Mac's eyes were fixed on the exit staircases hole in the platform above them. He glanced at the pallet, then down at the tent fabric in his hands.

"Poof." Mac sat on the ground, stared into space, and tried to come up with a plan.

Within minutes the grounds around the Cyclone had become unbearable. Some fairgoers wandered indiscriminately, only to realize that their life had been in danger all along. Occasional packs of people would try to sneak by only to be broken up when one of them exploded. The survivors, unable to run for the exits, would hide or run for the far corners by the lake. The farther back they ran, the less their likelihood of living out the night.

The Bagman stood with his jaw in his hand, contemplating the scene, trying to improvise himself out this mess. Mac had never been on a military battlefield, but when he looked up at Crankshaft, he realized it must be a lot like this. Here they were, entrenched, wanting to strike, but with no plan. Their only option, other than waiting, was charging into the jaws of death.

Meanwhile, he could hear the suffering; the screeching of the wounded, and the moans of the dying. The people of Chicago, his troops, were like soldiers caught in the barbed wire between front lines; some praying for release, some only for death.

Mac pulled out his pocket knife and began prying at the top of one of the paint cans. "Got a brush?"

Chapter 20
RUNAWAY TRAIN

The man who had been Conrad Wilcox was happy, genuinely, for the first time in ages. Anchored atop the highest peak of the rollercoaster, power surging up from the tracks into him, he didn't hate the past anymore. The future no longer scared him. From on top of the Cyclone people looked small. So small, that he didn't fear them anymore. In fact, he realized they didn't matter at all. They were part of the past. The dead burying its own. The future was now, and this moment belonged to Resonance.

His plan to extort millions from the World's Fair hadn't yet been defeated, but even if he didn't get the money, he was happy. Happy he wasn't giving up. He rationalized his gift of death. It didn't matter what happened to him, only that it never happened to a genius such as himself again. He didn't care what happened now. He would show them. All of them.

Flames popped and faded across the Midway, pushing tufts of smoke like pylons up into the air forcing the crowds around the wreckage toward the lake on one side, toward the exits on the other. Resonance twisted the dial on one of his wrists and curled it in front of him. Glass exploded, and the front of the Temple of Mystery collapsed. People screamed, trapped within. Resonance could listen to that sound forever.

Still, no matter how blissful he thought he was, something kept nagging at his subconscious. It seemed to flash subliminally across his mind when he least wanted it to. Then it hit him.

It was that man. The one in the mask. The Bagman.

He would have admired him, if the penny ante gangster wasn't such an ass. Smiling and joking, not even a care. Who the hell was he to laugh at Resonance? Who the hell was he to laugh at anybody? Some nut with a bag on his head. Running around and causing trouble, obstructing him, getting in his way. A stray dog that knew nothing.

Conrad didn't stop to think that the stray dog kept beating him. No, the man who had been Conrad Wilcox, instead, finally knew why he was standing atop the greatest rollercoaster in the world. It was destiny. It was going to happen. He was going to wait. He was going to guard The Cyclone.

And he was going to kill The Bagman.

140

Mac felt another chill run through the base of his skull. Almost like a breeze, but it was still hot outside. He told himself it was the paint Dr. Stoyer and Crankshaft had slathered all over him and his brand new suit. He hadn't let them paint the mask; he didn't know why. Still, he was going to miss that suit.

A gray man stood before the doctor and the ace mechanic, glistening where he hadn't dried yet. He had his hat in one hand, and was painting the outside of it to match the rest of his wardrobe. The gray Bagman took two steps and picked up the wooden pallet.

"Crank, can you do me a favor?"

Crankshaft gave him a low lidded look while raising his eyebrows, then inhaled and sighed.

"We need to paint one side of this pallet, so we can get the cars on the coaster rolling."

Crankshaft understood what he meant. They'd paint the pallet, if Resonance hit it with his sonic guns, it would catch fire, but they wouldn't. What Crankshaft pretended not to understand was that Mac wanted him to go, too.

"While you're getting the cars rolling, I've got to figure out a way to get upstairs and take this sucker out," Mac said.

"So while you're figuring it out, I'm the one that might just get popped." He stuck his head back up toward the staircase as if he was peering out of a bunker. The old veteran's silhouette in the flashing of the lights and fire brought to mind the soldier he'd been on the Western Front. "The paint's gray. It will work as camouflage on the concrete and rocks around the train switch, but he's bound to spot it on the platform." There was a moment of silence. "If we leave the pallet as is, we can use it to hide ourselves all the way over the platform. Once you're over the platform, that 'Vipraintium' stuff will camouflage you around the rocks and concrete. You get back to the platform, you pick the pallet back up."

"No, *you* pick the pallet up," The Bagman said.

"Hold on, hold on." Crankshaft held a hand up and waved Mac off, but he wasn't arguing. He took off his windbreaker and tie. "It's my favorite jacket."

The Bagman didn't seem to enjoy slapping the paint on Crankshaft the way he normally would have. He didn't like the idea of getting Crankshaft killed. He was fidgeting, still trying to figure out how he was going to stop the Sonic Terrorist. Then his eyes drifted over the top of Mirella's Tent still bundled by his feet.

"Just get the rollercoaster running Crank, I'll take it from there." He rubbed his forehead with his hand and some of the wet paint on his cuff came off on his mask. "There's only one or two ways to get up there, and

I'm not hopping out of another plane."

Neither Crankshaft nor Hunts bothered to question. Crankshaft tilted the pallet over his head so he could make his way up the stairs. The roller-coaster's engineer stood several feet away eavesdropping curiously, trying to make up his mind about whether to run or not.

Hunts pulled a small pistol out of his ankle holster. "I'm going back out front, see if maybe there's something we can do from there."

"Telling the cops not to kill me would be a good start," the masked man said. A shot fired in the distance. Somebody else screamed.

Everybody made eye contact, and nodded.

Crankshaft headed up the staircase. He was holding the pallet from beneath with his right arm like a carpenter moving drywall, using it to shield him from Resonance, who stood a mere hundred yards to the right on top of the highest peak the Cyclone had to offer. Edging slowly out onto the platform Crankshaft held the pallet higher, shifting the weight from his hip and balancing it on his head to remain hidden. Then he just stood there.

If he moved too fast, Resonance would blow him to smithereens.

He glanced down at Mac. Mac looked at his watch, and tapped it with his index finger to signal he'd be back. Crankshaft stepped slowly forward.

The Bagman took off down the aisle beneath the platform. If he could get to the rollercoaster and then climb up the scaffolding without being seen he'd have no problem.

Well, it sounded simple enough, anyway.

Problem was, Resonance wasn't moving, and it was quite evident he was guarding the generator. But Mac's racing thoughts didn't stop there.

"...if not the entire ride, if not the Midway, if not the World's Fair, the city, the world..." He stopped when he got to "the city." No way was The Bagman letting this jerk take Chicago. Place was bad enough as it was. He paced back and forth outside the chain link fence beneath the awning.

Mac had no problem with the chain link fence. He had another name for chain link fences; ladders. But once he was over the fence he'd stand out like...well, like a man painted gray in a vacant lot full of blinking white lights. Then, even if he could make it to the bottom of the coaster and climb, all Resonance had to do was look down, and he was toast.

Once The Bagman was halfway up the scaffolding he'd be above the lights, but until then he'd be a target. Why did everything have to be so black-and-white all the time, Mac thought, just once why couldn't he fall into a decision instead of always having to decide the fate of the world on some con man's shell game?

The Bagman smiled beneath the mask and answered his own question: *Because the con man holding the shells always wins.* The simplest way to run the shell game gag is when the host holds his hand under the table and drops the pea over the edge as he moves the shells around. The only way to reach the top of the Cyclone was to be the pea.

He spun on his heels and ran back to the turnstile. Crankshaft was almost across the platform. From there he'd have to crawl behind one of the cars to reach the concrete block where the rollercoaster's train switch was located. Mac started to signal for him to come back and then changed his mind. He hated his friend and mentor risking his life, but Crank was already out there. The field was in motion.

Mac inhaled deeply and thought about his version of the old shell game.

He heard something scrape against the concrete, and realized Crankshaft had dropped the pallet. The Bagman took off his hat and came as close to the exit to watch as possible without being seen. Luckily, none of the rollercoaster's train's linked together in long units, but in sections of six cars apiece. Crankshaft rested on his haunches behind the first series of cars. Gradually he shifted position to resemble a sprinter at the starting line, and glanced as best he could around the back of the car.

A voice yelled, "Ya wanna resonate? I got your resonate right here!" And six shots rang out from the street behind them. It was Hunts doing his best to become a distraction.

It worked.

Resonance turned to face the taunt from across the street, his back toward The Cyclone's center courtyard. He stretched his neck searching, his head twisting to the right occasionally to keep an eye on the generator. He raised his arm, but then lowered it.

Mac breathed a sigh of relief when he didn't hear the Resonance Gun whirr and moan. He admired Hunts's ability to be a complete jerk and still not attract enough attention to himself to get killed.

That was Mac's job.

Crankshaft on the other hand, had used the opportunity to sprint ten yards where the circuit switch for the rollercoaster cars stood out in the open. Without even looking for death from above, he clenched the handle of the switch, jerked it forward and then yanked it back, locking it into position. Only after he'd hit the dirt did he glance up to check if he'd been seen.

Mac stood on the stairs, his gun cocked in his hand as Crankshaft crawled back toward the platform. Without time for thought, the big man jumped down the entire length of steps. Running back past the turnstiles, he ran another twenty yards then turned, and began running back *up* the alternate staircase. He heard the ominous whine and drone of the Resonance gun as he rushed back up the metal steps three and four at a time. Stopping just below the platform, he glanced to the left. In one motion Crankshaft hopped back up on the wooden platform and hefted the pallet above his head. Mac remained where he was; his entire motivation being to

...he clenched the handle switch...

draw fire from Crankshaft if the master mechanic had been spotted.

Crankshaft was too good for that.

Instead, he came down the steps at a quick pace with his arms over his head, the pallet lifting itself from his palms as its edges rested on the wooden platform above. He stopped at the bottom of the steps, dusted his hands off and lighted a cigarette. His eye sockets expanded and both eyebrows lowered into one when he saw the gray painted masked man coming back down the walkway toward him.

"I thought you had something really important to do," Crankshaft said.

Two of the rollercoaster cars rattled off each other. Crankshaft stiffened as if they had startled him a little. Wheels turned, metal clanked on wood.

"Yeah, sorry about that." Mac watched as the first train of cars pulled from the station. "If you've got any brainstorms now's the time. Otherwise I'm going to have to bluff the hell out of this one."

"When have you not?" Crankshaft clenched his cigarette in his hand and exhaled smoke out of his nostrils. "We both know you're trying to get to the top of the rollercoaster. Way you think, I'm guessing your best idea to get there is to walk right on up the tracks."

"Provided this guy doesn't destroy them."

The two gray men faced the track as the first tiny train pulled up and away. Crankshaft flicked his cigarette butt on the track for luck. The electric lights blinked as if they shorted out a second, flashing off and on in a disparate rhythm.

"You're really going to try it?" Crankshaft said.

"Don't think of it as a shooting gallery, Crank. Think of it as a shell game. You know how the shell game operates?"

"Some of those guys know sleight of hand."

"I don't." Mac kneeled on the steps, peeking through the cracks in the platform. The first train of cars shook and rattled its way up to the highest point. "All we can do now is wait and see."

Mac saw Resonance spot the first car. The Sonic killer played with one of the dials on his wrist, and the now familiar whines and hums cut across the lot drowning out the rollercoaster.

The first train of cars exploded overhead. Wreckage slammed the boards above them, and the two men beneath the platform ducked. Before the dust had settled, Mac stuck his head out in the open. Several cars from the rollercoaster train had been tossed on the platform and about the lot. The battered cars sat smoking from the friction of their crash. Above him, he could see Resonance still standing on the peak. The Bagman squinted, straining his eyes to see if all the tracks were still there.

Waiting for a puff of dust to disappear, he realized the outcome would be decided in the next few minutes. If Resonance was blowing up the tracks with the cars, then he was planning on killing himself. If he was planning on killing himself, then he'd want to go out with a bang. If he wanted to go out with a bang he would destroy any hope of escape to keep from being captured. Mac prayed Resonance would leave the track intact.

If Resonance destroyed the tracks, they were doomed though Mac would try to kill him before anybody else got hurt. He didn't think about it as much as feel it and accept it. No good or bad, no life or death. It was just the way it was. Lines formed around his eyes, and the ends of his lips just barely turned up.

Resonance had waited till the train was level with him to destroy it. The death wish may be there but he'd salvaged the tracks to give himself a way out. As long as the tracks remained, there was hope.

Crankshaft eyed the wreckage, then gave Mac a worried look.

Mac stared at the track as the second train of cars began to rattle. He picked up the bundle of cloth from Mirella's tent, and held it under his arm like a football. Then the two men stopped a moment and looked at each other, risking their lives, painted gray, covered in dust, and began laughing. At each other. At themselves. At the whole thing.

"So a piece of fancy-ass canvass is your secret weapon," Crankshaft gasped between breaths.

"Don't forget..." Mac held a finger up in the air like a used car salesman "...'Vipraintium'!"

They clutched their stomachs and laughed till they couldn't breathe anymore. They were delirious, until the second train of cars began to rattle past.

"This one?" Crankshaft asked.

"Doesn't feel right. The shell game, you make at least three passes." The Bagman picked up the wooden pallet and wrenched a board off. He pitched it across the platform as a test to see how close Resonance was watching. Nothing exploded...yet.

The train of cars seemed to travel slowly, if at all. The waiting was unbearable, but the longer they had to wait, the better The Bagman's plan. This time, Resonance waited until the train was only one hill away. He aimed a wrist and the Resonance gun directly at the cars. The train shook, but not the tracks. The sound of ripping metal tore through the park. A few seconds later, more cars crashed and slid across the lot scattering sparks and scarring the earth in a path a hundred feet long.

For a second, the fairgrounds seemed strangely silent. No whoops or hums, only the occasional crackle of the burning exhibits and a single cry for help. The next train rattled across the track toward the platform. Mac pitched the top of Mirella's tent into the third car like he was throwing a forward pass. Nothing exploded. Peeking through the platform floorboards, he could see that Resonance was treating the rollercoaster cars as some kind of temporary diversion. He watched the generator and the lot around it more than the platform.

"Third time's the charm." Wedging his hat on, The Bagman hurtled up the steps and dived across the platform into the same rollercoaster car he'd thrown the top of Mirealla's tent. Rather than glancing up to check, he counted on the fact that if he had been seen, he was already dead. Not exploding or bursting into flame seemed to be a pretty good sign.

Crankshaft gave him the thumbs up from undercover, then went looking for a better place to fight from. Mac stayed curled around his bundle, facing the front of the car.

With every *clickety-clack* of the track up the first hill, Mac began to sweat a little more. The biggest worry was Resonance. If he was concentrating on some sort of plan they might be OK, but if he got playful and decided to work on his sharp-shooting…Chicago would be minus one criminal hero. The man with the bag over his head kept muttering something about the "third pass" and how it always worked. He didn't sound like he believed a word of it.

Mac hated the odds. It was so hopeless Crankshaft hadn't even bothered to needle him about his plan. The car rolled down the first hill, through a tight turn at ground level, and began to climb again. All Mac could do was hold on. For the first time, he realized the high tier Resonance stood on was also the third hill.

"Third time's the charm, the lovely lady loves the third pass," he kept repeating under his breath. As the chain clanked for the first part of the climb pulling him toward certain death with every link, The Bagman glanced over the front of the coaster car. Resonance was waving one hand in the air casually as if he were conducting a symphony, his eyes still on the generator.

Mac grabbed the bundle from Mirella's tent and wrapped himself around it in an effort to stay hidden. With his head down, he began mumbling to himself, counting down from ten to one. Every second encompassed an hour of mental anguish. When he counted one, without looking, he stood up.

Resonance remained in the center of the track smiling a good thirty feet away. As the cars strained to *click* their final *clack*, the coaster neared its peak. As the train came nearer, Resonance raised his sonic cannon and aimed at The Bagman.

Gunfire sounded from below in the street.

Mac already had the top of Mirella's tent winding up in one hand. He threw it hard, like a football. Spiraling in the air, the twenty feet of fabric spread out like a net. Resonance reacted, forcing the sonic terrorist to jump back and dodge the ever-widening net of fabric. With his plan suddenly at risk, Resonance fired his wrist cannon.

The coaster flew off the tracks, vibrating in the air just missing the sonic killer as it shredded into spare parts across the vacant lot. Scrap metal rained down on the courtyard and in the street below.

The Bagman was nowhere to be seen.

Chapter 21
SHOWDOWN ON THE CYCLONE

Resonance clawed the top of Mirella's tent from his shoulder and scanned the sky, looking for the hero in the falling wreckage. All he saw were the wheels flying off dismembered coaster cars. Maybe The Bagman had popped in the commotion. Maybe he was just plain disintegrated.

The villain turned, his eyes scoured the street and saw only the scattered throngs of tourists. Facing the courtyard, Resonance could have sworn he saw another man painted the same shade of gray. He raised his arm to fire the Resonance gun, but a volley of gunfire from the other direction gave him no option but to concentrate on his force field of sound. By the time he'd aimed back at the platform, the other gray figure was disappearing into the Irish Village.

The gray man was gone. But there was no way The Bagman could've been tossed to the platform, when the car he'd been riding in had wound up across the lot. He had to be dead.

Resonance's mouth widened and he began to smile. He watched as the second gray man across the street joined another man in the Irish Village. This gray man wore a different hat, reflective goggles, and he looked smaller than the big goon Resonance had faced earlier. No, he had hit him. And if The Bagman wasn't dead, he was wounded and probably dying. The smile narrowed to a grin of malevolent acceptance.

Resonance didn't realize the men shooting at him from across the street were friends of The Bagman's. He hadn't even realized yet that every time he'd started to look directly around the coaster, the two men fired more to distract him.

❋ ❋ ❋

Thirty feet below, hanging from the scaffolding in the shadows, The Bagman held on for dear life. Legs flailing in the air, leather-clad hands clung to the Cyclone's steel reinforced frame. He swung back and forth, got a leg up on one of the wooden beams and crouched in the darkness like a Chicago gargoyle catching his breath.

As he'd thrown the top of Mirella's tent, The Bagman had leaped for the beams below the track. He'd barely managed to get a grip on one of the steel shafts reinforcing the wooden frame. He'd almost pulled his shoulder out of the socket, but he had managed to land in between the lights and the top the Cyclone.

The situation was such that nobody was shooting at The Bagman for once. The police couldn't show themselves for fear of being vaporized and had been reduced to a game of hit and run. The National Guard, called in from Navy Pier, had stationed armory machineguns on the building across the way, but the men manning them were no longer there.

Hunts and Crankshaft had saved his bacon. Next time they might not.

The Criminal Detective slung one hand over his head and his palm lopped onto the metal frame above him. He wedged his foot in the corner below and kept pushing up. For someone who'd grown up breaking and entering it was like a kid's jungle gym, a bar to climb every four feet. Mac swung from rung to rung like a gorilla, twenty feet up, and then crouched again.

He saw the cables, two electric cables running up from the track directly to Resonance's torso. There was a lump on the terrorist's back beneath his shirt, probably some sort of regulator. Mac wasn't an electrician, but he knew how to pull a plug.

The sounds of normal life at the World's Fair had all but died. The crowd had left, or was leaving, for the most part. Aside from the occasional scream of a scattered onlooker vacating and the occasional gunfire, the only other noises seemed to be the crackle and pop of the fires scattered on the Midway.

Resonance spun on one toe to keep an eye on the generator. Mac slunk between the rafters and under the track. He could hear the footsteps on the wooden boards between the rails. The sphere of energy around Resonance swelled and shrank. Sensing something, Resonance turned again. Mac didn't move.

It was moments like this that made Mac seriously doubt he was the King of Thieves and even if he was, he felt like he was trying to pick somebody's pocket from across the room. To reach the last rung of the "ladder," swing himself over, and around the wooden fences siding the rollercoaster track, and then fight Resonance hand to hand would not only require superhuman effort, it would be madness.

The Bagman clutched his hand to his forehead. His eyes rolled up, then closed. He wished he could pace. He couldn't see the electrical contacts where Resonance was plugged in. Was he plugged in?

Machinegun fire raked the sky. Small gauge, probably a Thompson and not the Coast Guard guns. The Bagman heard the familiar tones whine and whoop. Something across the street exploded. There was no way to tell where and how exactly Resonance was going to strike. It wasn't as if there was a ray shooting out of his arm or anything. He just aimed the gun strapped to the top of his wrist.

Mac hopped up on the last rung. The gunfire had been the diversion he needed.

Resonance spun on the platform at the top of the tracks once again. Mac could hear his feet scoot. He wedged his hat on and tried to peer through the one slot in the boards above. Nothing. He could see which way Resonance was facing, he could see the wires running up his back, but he couldn't see what he was going to do. And he had to stop it.

Machine gun fire sounded again. The sound came from the courtyard. Someone was trying to shoot out the generator.

Mac heard the next train of cars rattle up the track. Resonance cursed the human race. Mac heard the high pitched whine, and felt the rumble of the low tones he couldn't even hear. Both tones wavered, and the track shook as the two became one. The car ripped off the top of the tracks, blew apart in the air, and scrap metal rained down in the courtyard. Resonance had spared the track; which meant he had to be hooked up to it.

Gazing from behind, Mac decided he'd have to chance swinging over the rail. Still, he needed another diversion. He hated that people were getting killed. He knew it wasn't his responsibility. And now that Mirella had warned him that he was The Knight of Cups, he might just believe in something so strongly that it would get him killed. He remembered the woman who had unknowingly turned the switch on the Teletractor and pressed the vibrating machine to her rib cage. He remembered people, just people, exploding. For no reason.

Wrong place, wrong time, your numbers up, Buddy! The man in the mask thought about that while he waited. People that did evil, legally or illegally, hurt other people, knowingly and unknowingly. The people who murder, he thought about his own family, steal more than just one life. To do that without even thinking was... He couldn't find the words. It was just wrong.

Maybe a Knight of Cups is supposed to die for that.

He wished he had some sort of plan. Something. The whole situation was like TNT, you had to light it to see what happens.

"*Well, you probably burst into flame or vibrate till your head explodes,*" Mac thought.

He was debating death by vibration or flame, when machineguns fired from the courtyard near the generator. Bullets pinged and ricocheted around him. Great, now that he was right by the guy, they'd started shooting at him again. Mac couldn't stay in the line of fire anymore without doing anything. He wanted to just kill this guy and get it over with. One of them was going to die.

Mac swung his arm up and a leather glove gripped the bottom of the platform. Then, he heard the whine of the Resonance gun.

The orb of sound energy encasing the man who had been Conrad Wilcox wobbled, reflecting the scattered light left on the fairground. The light trembled, and the force field waned. Then suddenly, it began to expand.

Three shots rang out. And the sonic aura of power began to expand again. Mac physically shrank as the orb's glow hummed at the inside of his head. He held his hands out to guard his face as the ball of sound and light began to envelope him. The palms of his gloves where the paint had been worn off began to heat up. His head boiled in the unpainted mask. Wishing he were closer to the lagoon, now more than ever, falling from an airship sounded like a better way to go.

Then, as the sound and light swallowed him, the broiling seemed to subside. There was no vibration inside the sonic field. No heat. No nothing, but a big target in a green hat standing there waiting to take a punch.

The Bagman *was* the Knight of Cups, and the cause was worth it.

Mac grabbed the platform with both hands, and swung a leg up and over. With that he was kneeling on the platform. Resonance, distracted by the gunners, faced the other direction. Mac was right behind him.

The electric cables running to the track had been literally tied around the third rail. Mac unholstered his .45 and spun it around in his hand like a movie cowboy. He flipped his wrists and when the pistol stopped spinning he was holding it like a hammer. Resonance tilted his head as if sensing something and, slowly, almost cautiously, he began to turn around.

Mac came up from his kneeling position on the platform and clipped him in the side of the head with the revolver's butt. Resonance went down, and his force field went down with him, its reflection wavering then collapsing.

Mac pulled up the back of the terrorist's shirt, and found some sort of flat battery pack strapped there. With the leather gloves on, it took him less than a minute to untie the power cable from the rollercoaster tracks and go through the terrorist's pockets.

The Cyclone's generator shut off in the background. Mac glanced over his shoulder at another gray man in a driving cap waving to him from the courtyard. Crankshaft pointed toward the rollercoaster's gate then disappeared under the awning.

Mac took off his hat and waved it in the air. Something whizzed by his ear, and gunfire raged over the Cyclone. Bullets zipped and ricocheted around him. With no place else to go, The Bagman dived face down on the wooden platform between the tracks.

Between the police, the National Guard and everybody else, nobody knew what was really going on. All they knew was somebody had destroyed a good time and they were angry about it. So they were going to shoot at anybody this side of the freak show.

He'd taken out Resonance, and now they were going to kill him. *Thanks a lot, Knight of Cups! Nice knowing you, King of Thieves!* Mac cursed the fates and the fair. He cursed a lot.

Voices yelled back and forth amid the gunfire, some giving orders. The shooting diminished, then stopped entirely. Mac took a deep breath, raised his head from the floorboards of the Cyclone and looked up.

Resonance stood above him, his wrist extended, the Resonance gun's amplifier pointed at Mac's head.

Mac's guess was the people across the street had stopped shooting because they were more afraid of Resonance than they were of him. He jumped to his feet as the all too familiar hum around the villain began to glow.

"I unplugged you," Mac said, pointing at the track.

"Ever heard of batteries, Moron?" The killer's eyes glowed between narrowed slits. His right hand twisted a dial on his left wrist. His left hand twisted one on his right. He extended both arms and aimed his fists at The Bagman.

Mac could hear the whirr and buzz inside in his head; feel it inside his body. He held out his hands and could see the leather smoking. He pulled his hat down, but he couldn't block the sound. The cuffs at his ankles felt like they were on fire. He couldn't think. He was having a stroke. Clenching his stomach with one hand, The Man of Steal extended his arm. At the end of it was a snubnose revolver.

"I'm going to kill you," Mac said, and pulled the trigger.

Resonance flinched, even though he knew the bullet couldn't penetrate his sonic field.

He screamed when the bullet hit him.

"Who are you? What are you? You can't shoot me!"

He squeezed his fists and a hum hit Mac in the head. The Bagman's mask and hands were smoking. Going up in flames, he refused to show it.

"You're running on residual battery power, Wilcox. You're unplugged. Game's over." The Bagman took two steps down the track toward him, then held up a lapel with his other hand. "Y'know, I slapped some of this glitzy new paint on some of my bullets. Supposed to absorb sound. Didn't think it would actually work, though."

Resonance's working arm reached out, aimed at The Bagman. The Bagman shot him in the other shoulder. Wilcox screamed. His eyes were wide and watering. He stomped his feet and roared, "I have a battery back up!"

"You mean these things?" Mac pulled out one of the batteries that had been in Conrad's back pockets all day. "Never let a masked man go through your pockets, Snappy. What're you, some kind of moron?" He slapped the side of his head, making sure his mask wasn't burning. It made him look crazier.

That's when Mac realized the hum in his head had faded. Resonance's batteries were drained. The Bagman would not go up in flames today.

The masked man took a step forward. Resonance tried to guard his face with his hands but he couldn't raise his arms. His shoulder's twitched, and the man who had been Conrad Wilcox saw something frightening in the eyes of his accuser.

The eyes in the darkness of the fabric did not shift, they didn't waver. They reflected the scattered light of the city, but there was something else there, something more than just righteous anger, something more than a feral gleam. Resonance stared at the eyes, backing away. Then, his own eyes went wide, and his lips quivered. He had recognized that look in The Bagman's eyes. He was staring into the eyes of a predator.

Resonance shifted his feet and backed up, hands waving at his sides. "You said you wanted a cut earlier. I can get you money! Whole nations!"

"You're gonna conquer whole nations, and you can't take down one cheap Chicago hood." Mac took a step.

Resonance kept backing away, but he was backing toward a roller-coasting forty foot drop. His voice was weak. "D-d-don't-don't you want to know why?"

"No. Not really." The Bagman paused in his tracks like he'd forgotten something. He pulled on the cuffs of his gloves so they'd fit tight, and made big leathery fists out of his hands. "You wanted something. You couldn't have it. So you killed innocent people. Doesn't sound real reasonable, does it?"

Resonance flinched backward and closed his eyes. Losing his balance on the steep coaster, he teetered on one foot at the edge of a four story drop.

The Bagman popped him in the nose, a hard jab, no wasted motion. Resonance stood off balance at the precipice, his arms waving to keep his balance as he began to topple over. The Bagman reached out with one hand and grabbed him by the lapels, saving him from the long painful fall, then held him there with his collar in his fist, his granite blue eyes burning into the sonic terrorist's soul. The Bagman broke eye contact only to shake his head to-and-fro, smiling beneath the mask.

Then he opened his hand.

Resonance bounced down forty feet of wood, nails, and rivets between the rails, screaming until the next bounce knocked him unconscious. It was the best sound Mac had heard all day.

The masked man stepped back from the rollercoaster's drop and took a breath, realizing how close he was to suffering the same fate. Spinning on his heel, he ran down the tracks in the other direction, away from the phalanx of policemen advancing across the street toward the Cyclone. Instead of plummeting, though, he leaned back slowing himself with one leather clad hand, holding the other out at his side for balance and slid down the rollercoaster's rails. When he hit the curve at the bottom, he popped up on the rail like he'd just slid into second base.

Mac didn't have time to make an escape. But he had to try.

An army of cops had just seen what had happened and without Resonance around, they still wanted The Bagman. Running across the Cyclone's platform, he was already shedding his coat and hat. He shoved them in a trash bin by the wall, and shoved his mask into his pocket. It wasn't as if he'd be unrecognizable. He still had paint all over his chest and tie.

As if he'd planned it all along, Mac rolled sideways off, and under the platform. Crawling beneath it on his hands and knees he steered away from the direction of the fighting. At the far end, he kicked two boards out of the side of the platform, and strode briskly for the shadows.

Chapter 22
THE GETAWAY

When Crankshaft, Coco, and Hunts walked into The Heidelberg Inn two hours later, the joint was almost jumping. Decorum required that after the disaster at the fair the band didn't play anything too fast, but that didn't keep them from laying out some melodies to celebrate by. Chicago had a long history of losing and winning, and they had both lost and won that day. But the city also had a long history rebuilding, and they always rebuilt. It was the sort of thing it might take a Cubs fan to understand. Chicago was always getting ready for next year.

The ace mechanic and his girlfriend arrived dressed in white. Crankshaft had borrowed a tuxedo from one of Coco's musician friends and she had put her designer white gown back on. Hunts was in his usual gray suit. The crowd applauded as they entered, for Coco, not the guys. As far as they knew the men were just hangers on.

The trio steered through the late night club crowd toward the dance floor, and saw Mac McCullough sitting in the shadows with a beer. Hunts stomped over. Crankshaft sidled. Coco flowed.

"Nice suit," Crankshaft said, to Mac.

"Thank the good tailor in locker 383, Security, Hall of Science," Mac said, toasting with his glass. "The gentleman was kind enough to use a really cheap padlock."

"Thought you'd be home in bed by now..." Crankshaft said aloud, then covered his mouth with the back of his hand. "...or in the hospital! What are you doing still here?"

"After tonight's little escapade I figured there might be some advantage to being spotted. The cops say they shot The Bagman."

"What else do they say?"

"That I'm one hell of a shot. Resonance is still alive but in a body cast, and a lot of pain, over at Cook County Hospital. He'll get the chair for this. I'm just glad I could give him some time to think about it before they pull the switch. Besides, I had to hang around for something."

"What?" Crankshaft asked.

"When I see it, I'll tell you."

"Sure, you will." Crankshaft took Coco's hand and headed back towards the dance floor. Hunts ordered a beer and sat down by Mac. Mac eyed the cops in the back of the room, then scanned the front before he said anything to Hunts.

"You find out what happened to the Black Wolf?"

"You're probably the only one in town who doesn't know, Mac. The Wolf landed that plane right in the middle of Wabash, and took out a gang of Nazi's at the Medinah Temple."

"Fascists…" Mac almost muttered to himself. He smiled a tired smile, happy that the Granton City Avenger was still alive to defend the defenseless. "Y'know, he seems like a much nicer guy than when I met him in New York."

"When you met him in New York you were selling fake oil wells and pulling the old fortune teller routine. I think things might have changed a little since then."

"A lot," Mac said. He waved his hand at the bartender for another round. "Crankshaft tell you about our Gypsy friend Mirella?"

"Already did a check on her. She runs some kind of *bodega* on the edge of Greektown."

"The kind of place you can pick up a crucifix, holy water, and a wooden stake to drive through a monster's heart, I reckon," Mac answered.

"Kind of place that's only open by appointment," Hunts said. "Nobody's home."

"Figures. Whoever she is, she's good." Mac sat his mug on the bar and stared at it a moment. "If she's not running a con she should be."

"And what are you still doing here, you dope?" Han's said. "Ain't you ever heard, the criminal always returns to the scene of the…"

"'Said' criminal saved the fair, Hunts. Thus, he's not a criminal. But don't talk so loud about it." Mac pointed with his jaw at the cops lined up by the rear wall.

Detective Costanovitch had gathered the group of detectives in a corner, and began laying out some kind of clean up plan. They were still counting the dead. Mac's head dropped backward, falling asleep. He slapped himself on both jaws, to stay awake, then waved a hand and ordered a coffee.

"You going to be able to make it, Mac?" Hunts said. "You look worn out."

"I'll be OK. Just waiting for something."

"Do me a favor, hang around ten minutes, and I'll be back with the best deal of your life!"

Mac's head fixed itself behind his shoulders. His eyebrows curled in curiosity. Seeing as how Hunts was a guy that could sell snow to an Eskimo, he'd gotten Mac's interest.

Mac nodded and Hunts ran out of the club.

That same moment, a young detective entered the club from the rear entrance. Costanovitch stood up from his table of detectives. The young plainclothesman was carrying the suit jacket and tie Mac had thrown away back at the rollercoaster. Costanovitch wrenched them from the budding detectives grip, and threw them down on the table. The detectives with seats sat down, the others gathered in the periphery.

Mac put his coffee down and idly began to circle the room, sneaking up behind the Detective Lieutenant.

"That's all you've got?" Costanovitch picked up the hat and began to inspect its lining. "Size seven and three quarters, label from Carson's." He narrowed one eye and gingerly picked up the suit by its back collar, not touching the paint. He looked inside the lapel for the size and manufacturer and smiled when he saw the stub of a dry cleaners ticket still stapled there. That meant they might be able to trace the suit to a local cleaner. His eyebrow lowered again, and his head jerked backward in sudden recognition. His face went blank for a second. Then he growled.

"This is my suit! That son of a bitch stole my suit!"

The whole back room broke into laughter. Mac had always thought he and Costanovitch were about the same size.

Detective Costanovitch gritted his teeth. His jaw clenched and shoulders rolled. He muttered, "Stole it right out of my locker."

Mac had suspected all along the suit belonged to the big detective. He'd known it was part of some practical joke even as Mirella gave it to him to wear. He tried to figure out if there was some sort of message there, but all he could come up with was that when you stole, you needed to be responsible for who you stole from. He made a mental note to himself to leave a nice pinstripe suit in Costanovitch's car when the detective wasn't around. Mac had broken a big case for Costanovitch today, but the obstinate lieutenant with the disarming manor was like a land mine waiting for The Bagman to step on it.

And him finding out The Bagman had been wearing his suit wasn't as funny as Mac thought it would be, either.

He shrugged his shoulders. Whoops and whistles suddenly came from the front room of the Hoffbrau house, sweet music with chimes and women's voices. Mac couldn't see around the partition into the nice part of the room. Whatever it was had nothing to do with him.

He was reaching for the back door when he felt a hand grab his shoulder.

"I thought you were gonna give me ten minutes?" Hunts said. "Listen, Mac, I know you're tired, but I've got somebody I'd like you to meet."

The crowd on the other side of the partition gasped and applauded as whoever it was walked toward the wooden partition. There was no way out. Mac shrugged his shoulders and wiped the palms of his hands. A dame walked around the corner, but not just any dame.

"Mac, I'd like you to meet Miss Sally Rand." Hunts waved a hand behind himself and bowed, presenting the world famous burlesque dancer as if he were introducing royalty.

To Mac, she was.

They sat down with four other people at a table in the corner, away from the dance floor. Evidently, Miss Rand had been playing to the crowds all day and needed a little time away from the center stage. After a while the music faded into the background. People began to discuss the things they had seen and been through that day. There were tears, and laughter. Policemen got off duty but never left. Two A.M. came and went and the bar stayed open. Soon there were toasts and dedications and singing.

Hunt's was jotting something in his notebook when he heard Sally Rand laughing and Mac said "Don't wait up." The public relations man finished working on his story for tomorrow, and looked around the room. He'd been looking for a story about hope, and even if The Old Heidelberg Inn was just a dive disguised as an exhibit, it was part of that story. There was hope, there had to be. Wait till next year.

It didn't strike him until a minute later that Sally Rand had left the club, too. Hunts slapped the bar and smiled, then, laughing, he ordered a round of drinks for everybody. Nobody else had noticed, but The King of Thieves had just slipped out the back door with the Queen of The World's Fair.

-THE END-

ABOUT OUR CREATORS

Author

BYRON CHRSTOPHER BELL - is the author and creator of *Tales of The Bagman*, Chicago's very own pulp hero. He has also written Airship 27 Adventures for *Secret Agent X*, *Jim Anthony: Super-Detective*, and the first volume of *Dan Fowler G-Man* adventures. An award winning short-story writer, Bell is currently working on a tribute to Black Mask Magazine pulp writer Paul Cain's novel *Fast One*. He is lucky to live with his wife in "the city where the weak are killed and eaten."

Join him on Facebook, or at his weblog: http//chicagobagman.blogspot.com

Interior Illustrator

ANDY FISH - is a 16 time graphic novelist, writer and artist. He is also the author of a series of how to books from Quarto Publishing in London and a series of Graphic Novels from McFarland Press in North Carolina. His latest book is DRACULA'S ARMY, due in stores Halloween 2013.

Andy's fine art work has been featured in art galleries all over the world and one of his paintings is in the collection of the National Gallery In Washington DC.

He currently lives outside Boston with his lovely wife Veronica and can be visited on the web at www.andytfish.com

Cover Painter

LAURA GIVENS - is a Denver Based author and artist. Her art has graced the covers of numerous publishers' books and magazines. She has provided illustrations for Orson *Scott Card's Intergalactic Medicine Show*, *Jim Baen's Universe, Talebones, Science Fiction Trails and Tales of the Talisman*. Her work may be viewed at www.lauragivens-artist.com. In 2010 she naively decided she could probably write stories as good as many she had illustrated. She has sold works ranging from zombie stories to space operas. She was co-editor and contributor to *Six-Guns Straight From Hell*, a weird western anthology, and is art director for *Tales of the Talisman* magazine.

CRIME IN THE CITY

In the middle 1930s, Chicago was one of the fastest growing metropolises in the country. Situated on mighty Lake Michigan, it was the home to millions of hard working Americans looking to a better themselves. The Windy City was also shackled by its bootleg history, a time of violent gang wars that had permanently established a brutal underworld empire second to none. Corruption was the order of the day and both the police and government were in the pay of the mob bosses.

Frank "Mac" McCullough was a foot-soldier in one of the city's toughest families until he was ordered to rough up his uncle—a decent man with a gambling problem. The innate decency in Mac rebelled and suddenly he found himself up against the very men he had once admired and followed. Determined to put an end to their lawlessness, Mac put a bag over his head as a crude disguise only to become labeled *the Bagman* by the press.

Now writer B.C. Bell tells the amazing stories of old Chicago's most unique hero. Aided solely by a tough, black WW I veteran named Crankshaft, Mac wages war against the mob in fast-paced, non-stop action tales pulp fans will cheer. Featuring nine illustrations by Kelly Evereart and a cover by Laura Givens. Airship 27 Productions is thrilled to present pulpdom's newest avenger,

THE BAGMAN.

A NEW Pulp Hero in Old Chicago!

AN AIRSHIP 27 PRODUCTION

CORNERSTONE BOOK PUBLISHERS

PULP FICTION FOR A NEW GENERATION!

LINKS FOR OUTLETS AT : AIRSHIP27HANGAR.COM

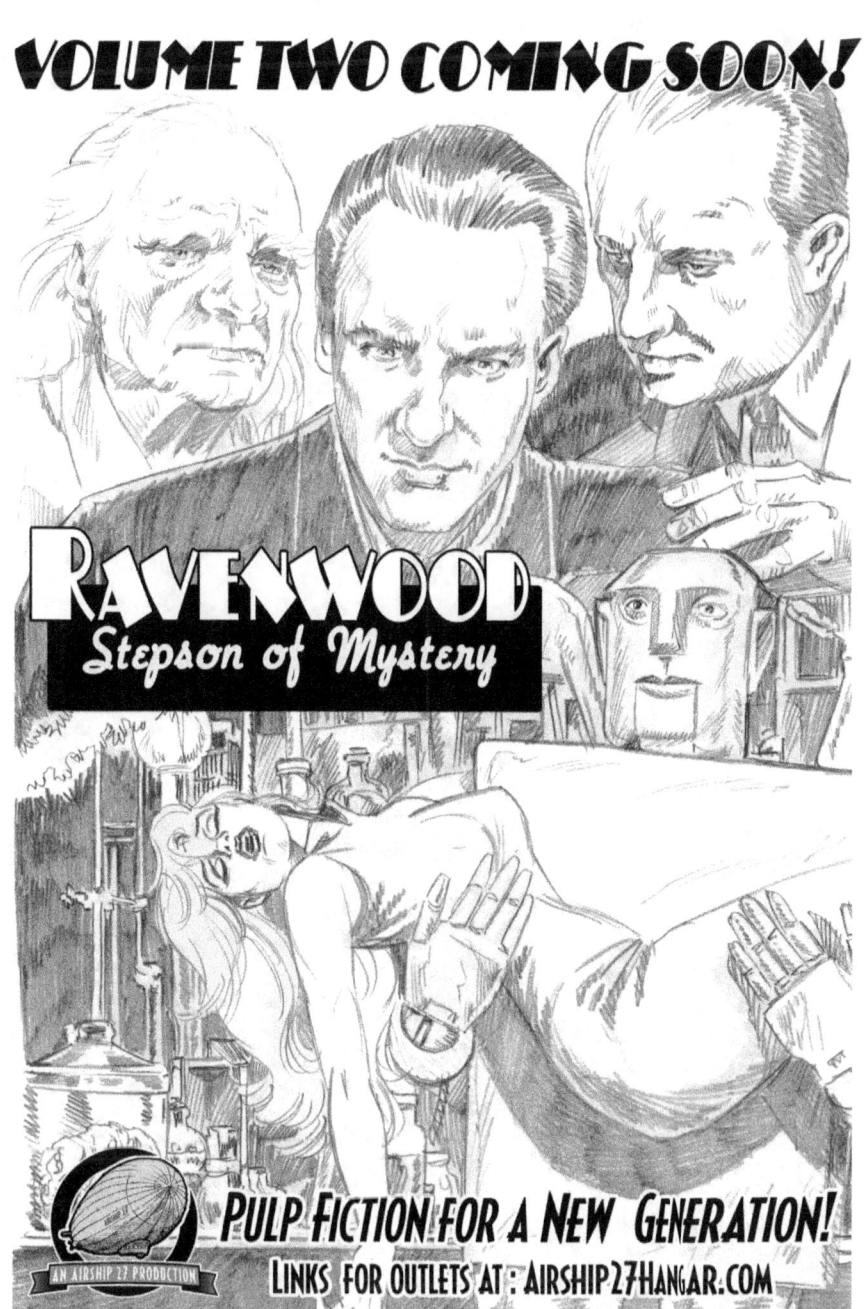

www.ingramcontent.com/pod-product-compliance
Lightning Source LLC
Chambersburg PA
CBHW071241250626
47163CB00001B/283